I0571327

A Sherlock Holmes Sextuplet: Six Sherlockian Pastiches

Written by David Francis Curran

Introduction:

Although I have an Irish name, my background is Irish on my father's side and English on my mother's. On my mother's side, one of my great-great-grandmothers, Trudy (I don't know how great she actually was; the family records were partly destroyed in a flood) had been a contemporary of Sir Arthur Conan Doyle's. A spiritualist, Trudy, had done him some great favor for which he had given her some original manuscripts. At the time, "The Final Problem" had been published, and Doyle felt himself free of Holmes. By the time he started writing Holmes again, Trudy had died, and her possessions had shipped off to America with her only son—another great-great-grandfather.

Apparently, this son had written Doyle asking if he'd like his manuscripts back. The son, who was my namesake, was a big fan of Doyle's, whose favorite Doyle story was the Lost World. I do not know what he wrote to the author. It may have been that Doyle, considering Holmes not to be his most important work, appreciated a fan of his other writing. In any case, Doyle began to correspond with him. One story here was from a letter Doyle sent David. Apparently, one day not long after the spy Von Bork had been dealt with, a young lad approached Holmes and Watson as they visited the beach at Blackpool Sands. The lad, whose name was Anthony Pratt, was with his family, which was on an attempted last holiday before the world war made such holidays impossible. It may not be a coincidence that this same lad in 1944 patented a game to be played in the bomb shelters during WW II called Cluedo. This game, today, is known as CLUE. His story is included below as Colonel Mustard's Secret.

These manuscripts were found in my most recent grandfather's possession.

David Francis Curran April 2018

The Adventure of Miss Stephanie Ray

I confess that as Sherlock Holmes' chronicler, I have kept my dissertations to the study of his professional interests and have stayed well out of our private lives. However, the story I'm about to relate does concern a matter of deep personal emotion on my part, and, until presently, I have found it quite challenging to lend to my readers. The tale does, however, show the profound genius and certainty with which Holmes managed to conduct his investigations, and it was this experience, which compounded my admiration and friendship for him.

It was the first summer of our lodging together. Holmes, sitting by the open window overlooking Baker Street, seemed to be absorbed in the tortuous paths of the smoke issuing from his pipe into the afternoon air. Knowing as little as I did about him at that time, I postulated he would care no more for the direction of fumes than he did for the fact that the earth circled the sun. Holmes had, at the time, won my admiration in the case I call A Study in Scarlet, in which I took a small part and which I have already published. At least

I felt him an interesting companion, although his egotism bored me. Even if his theories were sometimes correct, I must admit that his attitude forced me to feel the role of a physician slightly more sensible and important than that of a private inquiry agent. I was seated in my chair by the fireplace reading the Times; though, I didn't find much that amused me. It was a long, dull day, and my thoughts occasionally drifted to starting my practice again. Leisure time was beginning to get on my nerves, and a certain young lady with whom I had a dinner engagement had stirred in my mind thoughts of matrimony.

It was as I sat meditating that Holmes turned and broke in on my train of thought, querying, "What time are you to meet the young lady for your theater engagement? "

"Half-past-seven," I said and suddenly realized that I had not told Holmes of my plans for the evening.

"Surely, Holmes, you haven't been so bored as to have been spying on me?" I demanded.

"Nothing of the sort, Watson," he said, turning away from the window and facing me with a grin. "It's just the logical conclusion from a given set of facts and observations formulated into a workable theory."

"Preposterous!" I exclaimed, feeling spied upon and expecting in the least an apology for the intrusion. I did not mind Holmes knowing of my plans. I simply hadn't mentioned them, because he was himself a misogynist and he seemed to care too little for anything that resembled polite conversation.

"Not preposterous at all, my dear Watson," Holmes answered calmly, his eyes shining with the look of a chess player whose opponent has just walked into a mating trap. "You, yourself, might have been aware of the pieces of information you have put before me, but, as you have not trained yourself to observe, they have gone unnoticed by you. Therefore, you could not possibly see how I drew a conclusion from them."

"You don't expect me to believe that you inferred my taking a lady to the theater from these theories of yours? "

"Precisely, Watson, precisely."

"Well, frankly, Holmes, I don't see it."

"Tut, tut, Watson; before you forego our friendship of what it is, shall explain how I made these deductions."

He relit his pipe with an ember from the fireplace and continued. "The part concerning the theater was quite simple. Yesterday you went for a walk before lunch. On returning, you went out again right after lunch, this time taking a carriage, indicated by the spots of mud on your coat sleeves. When you returned again, your boots were covered with clay found only in the vicinity of one local theater. Indicating that during your walk, you found a reason for a second outing, and, during the second, you had a particular errand: theater tickets."

"But surely Holmes, not even you can tell at a glance that it was mud from in front of one particular theater? "

"Very simple, Watson. I knew you took a cab. When one takes a cab, they most likely take it directly back again. Therefore, the only mud on your shoes would come from the location of your destination. The theater is the only place where you can acquire mud in your instep with ticket paper in it."

A broad smile crossed his face as he said this, and the simplicity of his reason annoyed me. I thought of a way I might catch him.

"Oh, yes, " I said. "Well, how can you be sure I bought tickets? Did you go through my pockets? I didn't show any to you."

"Elementary, my dear Watson. You are a creature of habit. In the months we've been together, you haven't once gone out of your way for anything. The only things you might have gotten in the vicinity of the theater that you couldn't have gotten elsewhere are theater tickets for this week's show."

"But how did you know it was tonight? And how did you know it was a young lady I was taking?" I asked, quite flustered. That my secrets and personality had been analyzed like one of Holmes' test tubes caused my ire to rise.

"The young lady was merely conjecture, however, correct. All the facts pointed to your taking a lady out. When this morning, you left your shaving utensils by the window, I knew something was afoot. Obviously your not putting them away was an indication that you intended to shave again, and not merely an oversight, for your putting your utensils away is more than a habit with you. Now, if you were going with a gentleman, I don't think you would shave twice for him; otherwise, I would expect you to shave for me twice a day. As to the theater, I could not imagine anywhere else you would take a young woman on your first engagement, as there aren't any concerts or such this evening. I expect you will be asking Mrs. Hudson for the brown tweed you gave to her yesterday to clean for you? "

"Why, I almost forgot. Hm-m-m seems quite easy now that you mention it."

"You know, dear fellow, one would feel you hold your life with the opposite sex a secret from your fellow lodger."

"Nothing of the sort," I protested. However, I didn't carry the argument further. For his feeling was correct. I would not, however, have appreciated Holmes' cynicism if I had mentioned it.

The matter was dropped. Later, when I left for my engagement, Holmes was absorbed in some chemical determination. My goodnight was responded to by an impersonal wave, which I have come to learn is a lot when he is deeply engrossed in a problem.

I'll never forget that moonless night. I hailed a hansom, and, as I rode, my thoughts were on the very smart young woman I was to escort to the theater. The thought never occurred to me; perhaps it was her charm that she lived in one of the worst parts of London.

As the hansom pulled up the street, I noticed there was a crowd of onlookers about the door. I told the driver to wait and made my way into the crowd.

"What is going on?" I asked a woman in the crowd.

"There's been a murder," she whispered in harsh cockney voice.

My mind went aflame; I jostled my way through the throng. A constable stood with the landlady, blocking the doorway.

"Now, where do you think you're going?" demanded the constable as I pushed by him.

"What's happened?" I gasped. Looking into the room, I could see that the place was a shambles.

"Now, what business is that of yours?" he asked, laying a restraining hand on my shoulder.

"My good man!" I was quickly losing my temper. "The young lady who lives here and I had an engagement this evening," I said, pushing off the constable's hand. "And I'm a physician. Where is she?"

The constable grasped me with both hands forceful-ly. I was about to give him my right hand when he said, "She's not here."

"Where is she, then?" I yelled.

"We don't know. The landlady found the door ajar and the place like this."

As I was at that point, just barely inside the door, I caught sight of something that gave me, even with my experience of the horrors of war, a sick feeling. There was a large pool of blood with a jagged broken bottle, edges covered with blood, lying in it. A thousand hor-rors passed through my mind. It was a moment before I regained my senses. The constable was speaking. I only caught the end of what he said.

"Now, why don't you sit tight until Inspector Lestrade gets here?"

"That fool Lestrade," I muttered. I could picture Lestrade in this case, concluding that I was the culprit. Although a fair police officer, having known him through Holmes, his lack of imagination and jealousy of Holmes did not impress me. My thoughts were only on finding the young girl and on the one man I hoped might be able to do it.

"Now, where do you think you're going?" demanded the constable, but I was out the door and through the crowd, which closed after me. This kept the constable momentarily from pursuit. I jumped into the cab and promised the cabby a half-crown if he got me to Baker Street in fifteen minutes.

Holmes was standing by the door as I rushed in, puffing, trying to catch my breath. "Watson, what is it? "

"Come quickly, Miss Ray has been --." Before I had the time to explain, Holmes read my tragedy.

"Come, Watson," he said, reaching for his hat and coat. "You can tell me on the way."

His actions gave me some confidence. I was never so grateful for the cool-headed powers of my colleague as I was that evening. We arrived back at the flat, barely a half-hour since I had left.

I related what had occurred as we rode in the carriage. Holmes listened attentively yet silently.

As we pulled up to the door, my heart pounded mercilessly. Onlookers still lingered about, hoping for the worst. I felt the deep pain of the afflicted in the sideshow humanity makes of their grief. Holmes paid the driver and dismissed him. As we approached the door, the small ferret-like figure of Inspector Lestrade emerged.

"Ah," Holmes said, "I see our friend Lestrade is already here."

"Mr. Holmes, Dr. Watson, what brings you here? Don't you think the official police can handle this one? How did you get here so fast?" asked Lestrade with a scowl.

"That's him," yelled the constable, now appearing on the doorstep. "That's him, the one who was here."

"You mean Mr. Holmes," exclaimed Lestrade, gesturing toward Holmes.

"No, the other," he said, running up and taking hold of my arm. "This one."

"I say!" I exclaimed, shaking off his grip. The Inspector gave me a stern look.

"You were here, Dr. Watson? "

"Yes," I said solemnly.

"Well, Dr. Watson, what were you doing here?" asked Lestrade. "Speak up, man."

"Sir, surely," said Holmes, "you don 't expect to arrest Watson? "

"Yes, indeed," I said. "Try to keep a civil tongue in your head, and don't treat me like a common criminal."

"Now see here," said Lestrade, slightly angered, "I'm only trying to do my duty. Not like some people fiddling around with elegant theories." He gave a sneering glance at Holmes. "Now, if you please answer my question."

"You'd better do as he says, Watson before he wastes more of our precious time."

"Well," I said, "I had an engagement this evening with Miss Ray. When I arrived, I found this officer here. I really must insist we start looking for her. The young lady might be in danger."

"You weren't here, by any chance, before that?" asked Lestrade.

"I assure you," said Holmes, "that Dr. Watson did not leave the flat all day until quarter-after-seven. We are wasting precious time, Lestrade."

The aggressiveness had gone out of Lestrade's manner. He looked at us somewhat beseechingly. Obviously, he had been having a hard time of late with the minor thieveries that plagued London.

"All right, Holmes. You can come inside if you like. I don't think you'll be able to do much on this one. It appears there's been a bit of a scuffle here and certainly a bit of violence."

As we entered, he indicated the corner of the flat between the overturned dinner table and the desk, where there was an immense puddle of blood, almost dry, on the bare floor. The whiskey bottle, it's bottom smashed, lay in the pool. Clinging to the edges were viscid droplets of blood.

Lestrade picked up the bottle. "It appears this was the weapon."

"Quite a horrible weapon, Inspector," replied Holmes. "One would imagine that its victim would shed a great deal of blood and rather geographically."

Holmes got down on his knees, and, for a few minutes, he examined the glass and the pool of blood before finally rising.

"Find anything interesting?" queried Lestrade haughtily.

"Perhaps," said Holmes. "Do you mind if I have a look around the rest of the flat?"

"Help yourself, Mr. Holmes. However, there are just two other rooms, and they are in as much of a mess as this one."

Holmes' examination of the other rooms took only a few minutes. When he returned, I could see a gleam in his eyes.

"Watson, please tell me how you met this young woman."

"Well," I said nervously, trying to collect my thoughts, for this whole affair had definitely shaken me. "It was yesterday morning during my stroll. I was just a few blocks from here. I noticed an attractive young woman with an older woman approaching me. The young woman was of medium height with long dark hair and blue eyes, and she was dressed in a blue-flowered dress. The older one was quite common looking, dressed in black, somewhat stooped over... oh, and she had a mole on her ear."

"Which ear was that, Watson?"

"The left, no the right. That's it, the right. I'm sure of it. She was facing me, but what of that?"

"Perhaps quite a bit, Watson; but, pray, continue."

"As they came up, the older woman started to faint. I rushed to their aid and offered my assistance as a physician. Since I couldn't very well tend to her on the street, I asked the young woman where she lived. She gave me this address, and, since it was nearby, I thought it best to call a carriage and bring her here. I was quite taken by the young woman's charm. During the entire carriage ride, she was quite grateful and attentive to me. Once we had arrived here, I helped the old woman, her mother, to that chair. After a spot of brandy, she seemed to improve magnificently. I learned that they were Mrs. Lloyd Ray and her daughter Stephanie. It was the young woman's flat and her mother was visiting. Miss Ray brought me tea, and the three of us had a most interesting chat. So outgoing and charming was Miss Ray, that before I left, I had made a theater engagement for this evening."

"You say there were two of them here tonight then, Dr. Watson?" asked Lestrade.

"No, no, Mrs. Ray was to leave this morning for Liverpool."

"I suggest," said Holmes, "that you try to locate Mrs. Ray in Liverpool, Lestrade." Holmes turned to me. "Come, Watson, we should be going. There's work to be done."

"You have a clue, have you?" asked Lestrade.

"Perhaps, but I prefer to follow my own clues privately until I am sure of their substance. I'll let you know if I turn anything up."

When we again were in the street, I noticed that the crowd had dwindled to only one or two.

"Let's walk, Watson," said Holmes. "It'll do you good and give me a chance to think. I suggest when we get back, you take a bromide and get some rest. This ordeal has been most trying for you. I have an important clue to follow, and if it turns up something, I may need you fresh tomorrow."

"Do you think there's any hope for Miss Ray?" I asked. The pressure had been building up since we returned to her flat, along with a feeling of hopelessness, and I much desired some encouragement from my colleague. The thoughts that had been raging through my mind! What unbearable fate had befallen the young lady I had just chanced to encounter? Worst of all, I felt in some way to blame for the tragedy. Perhaps my presence had pushed a desperate lover to an ugly act.

"You'll excuse me if I don't explain, Watson; but, I don't believe that the blood belonged to Miss Ray. We will part here. Go directly home and get some sleep. You'll need it for tomorrow. I am going to find the young lady's mother tonight."

"Won't the police take care of that?"

"I don't feel we should leave that up to the police. With luck, I will have hunted her up before morning."

With that, my friend disappeared into the night.

It was nine o'clock when I awoke. Holmes was up, sitting in his favorite chair and smoking his before-breakfast pipe.

"Good morning, Holmes. Any news?" I begged God for any hope.

"Don't trouble yourself, Watson, I believe that we will have the matter cleared up shortly."

"Don't trouble yourself! Holmes, I never believed you could be so callous. Here a young lady is violently attacked with such a horrible weapon as a broken bottle, and you say 'don't worry.' The poor young thing, if not dead, might be horribly disfigured."

"No, Watson. As I've told you, the facts do not point to her even bleeding much less being disfigured, so you need not worry about that."

He had told me the night before that he did not think it was the young lady's blood. But still, I had spent an almost sleepless night imagining the worst. His reconfirmation gave me blessed relief, for, in all the time I had been with him, I had seldom found him to be wrong. "Then you think the attacker was the one who was bleeding?" Yet I had no idea how he could tell who the poor unfortunate was who left that pool of spattered blood on the floor.

Suddenly a stone smashing its way through our window interrupted my chain of thought. Holmes and I both jumped up and gazed out.

"Watson, there," Holmes pointed to a figure, a man, tall and lean with a bowler hat, running down the street, turning and disappearing into an alleyway.

"What the devil is going on, Holmes? "

"What the devil is going on, Watson? What would bring a young gentleman of not so good financial grace to throw a stone through our window? But Hallo! What's this?"

Holmes bent and picked up the stone that lay now on our rug. A piece of paper was wrapped around the stone, tied on by some cord. Holmes quickly detached the note and held it up to the window so that we could both read the scrawled message.

Mr. Holmes,

Come alone, at once, to the corner of Duke St. and Manchester Square or your friend Watson will never see Miss Stephanie Ray again.

"No time to lose, Watson," said Holmes as he went for his cape.

"Do you want me to accompany you?" I asked.

"No, Watson, that would enrage the sender of this note."

"Yes, what am I thinking, Holmes! We can't allow the lady to be endangered more."

As I said this, for just a second, I thought I caught a faint glimpse of a grin on Holmes' face.

"Good luck, Holmes. Let's hope that this fiend doesn't harm her any more than he already has."

At that moment it occurred to me that we might have some part in the plot that Miss Ray's abductor had devised; but, before I could bring this to the attention of Holmes, he was already going down the steps and was, with a bang, out the front door. My thoughts that Miss Ray's abduction was in some way due to my alliance with Holmes put me in a state of agitation. I can't begin to tell you the feelings of guilt that raged in my mind. I paced back and forth through the room, recalling how I had met her, the pleasant hours we had spent together, her face, a vision of her smile in my mind. And then I heard a step on the stairway.

"Holmes back so soon?" I thought. As I turned toward the door, it burst open. In the doorway stood a young man of about six-and-twenty dressed in a dark grey suit. He was my height, but of narrower frame, with gleaming blue eyes and a crooked smile framed by a dark beard. He mightn't have looked sinister at all except for the Webleys No. 2, which he held in his right hand.

"Dr. Watson, it's a pleasure to meet you," he said cordially.

"Well, I can't say the same." I was confused by his manner and by the revolver. "You have the advantage, mister?"

"I believe, Doctor, I will keep the advantage." He spoke now in a more serious and sinister tone. I weighed the possibilities of jumping him as I waited to see what mischief was afoot.

"I wouldn't try anything foolish or try to con me into thinking your Mr. Holmes is behind my back. That little errand I sent him on will keep him occupied for at least a while." He chuckled and gestured toward the broken window.

"My God!" I gasped. The thought that this was the rogue who had brutally abducted that young lady roused every fiber of my being. It was all I could do to keep myself from pouncing upon the scoundrel despite the revolver.

"Just hold your temper, Dr. Watson. Now, if you don't want Miss Ray's death upon your head, you'd better cooperate."

The poise and cool of the scoundrel burned deep into my soul. The audacity with which he referred to her and Holmes had referred to him as a gentleman. If only Holmes . . . but, by God, together we would bring this scoundrel to justice. I took a deep breath and glared at the rascal, self-assured that shortly I would take part in repaying him for his crime.

"Well, get on with it, man. What do you want? "

"Glad to see you want to cooperate, Doctor. You've been living with Holmes for a long time---so you must know where he keeps his things, his records, etc."

"Well, so that's it! What is it you want that Holmes has?"

The man nodded. "There's a certain envelope in Mr. Holmes' possession which contains the records and notes of a certain Dr. Edward Casselman. It is that envelope I desire, Dr. Watson, and, if you value the life of that young lady, you'd better hand it over to me."

Casselman, I thought, the name was vaguely familiar, some case of Holmes' occurring before I came to share the rooms at Baker Street. It dawned on me that this man was too young to be the person in question and that he, therefore, must be one of his henchmen. The thought that I was betraying Holmes by helping

16

this ruffian to gain his ends grieved me. Still, my duty surely did lie in attaining the safety of Miss Ray. It occurred to me that I might substitute a fake document for the original. Still, the possibility of discovery was evident, and such a development might cost the life of the young lady.

"Well, Holmes keeps his papers in that desk," I said, pointing. "After you, Dr. Watson."

The thought again occurred to me that I could get the jump on him as he followed me to the desk. However, I reasoned that it would still be to no avail. I'd have the revolver, but he'd still have Miss Ray. I walked over to Holmes' desk, sincerely believing it to be locked, and, since Holmes carried the key with him, I expected I'd have to force it open.

"It'll be in the desk," I growled. "I imagine it's locked."

But as I reached for the lower drawer, to my astonishment, it opened. It was not like Holmes to forget to lock the desk, I thought. The drawer was a cluster of papers. I fidgeted around among the documents, and I noticed a large manila envelope. As I raised it out of the drawer, I saw the name of Dr. Edward Casselman on the flap. I realized that it is possible to vehemently hate someone just by seeing his or her name. For that is what I felt, hatred for a Dr. Edward Casselman, a planner, and schemer who had commanded the abduction of an innocent young lady.

Holding the envelope up toward the man, I queried, "Is this it? "

"Let's have a look, shall we?" he said, reaching with his left hand for the manila envelope. He snatched it away from me and glanced at the name.

"So it would appear. While I hope you don't take of-
fense at my parting so soon, I want you to know I am
grateful for your cooperation."

"What about Miss Ray?" I asked.

"Oh, the young lady. I forgot about her," he sneered.
"Well, if you're a good lad and don't get any fancy idea
s about following me, she'll be released in an hour."

I swear if I had had my hands around his throat at
that moment, I would have throttled him.

"Oh well, ta-ta, and don't forget about following," he
jeered wickedly.

He pocketed his revolver and turned toward the
door. At just that moment, it opened, and there stood
Holmes with his own revolver in hand. The rogue
stepped back, and Holmes entered.

"He's got a revolver in his pocket," I shouted.

"Get it, Watson," said Holmes smoothly.

Although I expected Holmes to have his reasons for
cornering the rascal, I was worried that his actions
might endanger Miss Ray. However, the rogue himself
brought up the question.

"If you don't let me go, it will go badly for Miss Ray,"
he said, yet somehow the power had gone out of his
voice.

"Oh, dear me, Miss Ray," chuckled Holmes, "I almost forgot about your wife. Won't you come in, young
lady?"

All I can say is that I was never so personally
shocked or felt a more mixed conglomeration of emotions as at that instant, when the young lady whom I
had been so grievously concerned about, stepped into
the threshold of our flat. Now dressed in a sweeping
black dress and wearing a black hat with a black veil
pushed up over her head, she rushed into the arms of
the young man who had just confessed to being her

captor. Most shocking of all, Holmes had revealed her to me to be the young man's wife.

I stood staring at her. Her face averted from me, buried in the chest of our prisoner.

"What is the meaning of this, Holmes?" I gasped.

"I hate to say this, Watson, but these two have used you as a pawn in their game of treachery, put up to it, I may add, by Dr. Casselman."

The young man looked at me and at Holmes, an overwhelming look of despair and fear in his eyes.

"What are you going to do with us, sir?" he asked of Holmes.

"I haven't quite decided yet. There are still some points I am not clear on," answered Holmes.

The young lady, at last, turned her head from her husband's chest. "John and I will tell you everything you want to know," she said, and to her husband, "I knew something like this would happen. I knew we'd get caught."

"Please take a seat," said Holmes, calmly now. He went over to the mantel, took down his clay pipe, and filled it from his Persian slipper. He then seated himself in his favorite chair.

"You don't mind if I smoke?" he asked the young lady. "No," she humbly replied.

"Suppose you two tell me, then," said Holmes, "How you became involved in this."

The young man hesitated before beginning. "My wife and I were just recently married. We moved to London from Liverpool and acquired a small room in a house on Weymouth Street. I had no position and was making the rounds. I hoped to get employment as an accountant for one of the brokerage houses, but I was having rotten luck.

I'd been looking for almost a month, and our small savings was nearly gone. On Friday last, it had been another rotten day with not even a glimmer of hope. So frustrated was I that I stopped in a pub hoping to enliven my hopes with spirits. In this pub, I met an older gentleman, a Dr. Casselman, though not a medical doctor, to whom, while I drank, I told my sad tale. To my surprise, he said that he might have a job for me if only for a short period, that would net me one hundred pounds. He told me that a certain Sherlock Holmes, a private spy (I noticed a slight twinge in Holmes' cheek at this.) had appropriated some papers of his and that he had devised a plan for regaining possession of them. He would set Steph up in a flat and arrange that she should meet Dr. Watson, a colleague of Holmes. Then, on an evening when Steph and Dr. Watson would be going out, he'd stage the flat as though Steph had been attacked and some horrible crime had been committed. After sending a note, and while Holmes was gone, I would approach Watson and demand the papers for the young woman's life. It was easy for me to believe in my intoxicated state, that Holmes was as evil as Dr. Casselman said and that what we were to do was correct.

"Casselman explained that no crime would be committed for there would be no abduction, and, once he had his papers back, Holmes would be helpless to reproach him as Holmes had obtained the papers illegally in the first place. I might add that I felt quite fearless when with drink, and I didn't consider any retaliation on Holmes' part. Of course, when I was sober the next day, the probability of Holmes being a scoundrel seemed less likely. Especially when the police might be called in on an abduction case. However, the one hundred pounds looked so good I decided to go on with the affair. He gave us some money for the flat and a jar of blood we were to sprinkle on the floor. The broken bottle was my idea."

"That's enough. We know the rest," said Holmes seriously. "You know, Ray, you've been playing a dangerous game. If you'd killed Watson here, I guarantee you, you would have hung. I might add that my colleague is quite a formidable opponent, and he might easily have killed you if pushed beyond control."

Holmes' words struck me deeply with respect for my ability, which he seldom put into words.

"It seems your plan and meeting were just as I had predicted," added Holmes.

"But how?" asked Ray.

"That, sir, is none of your affair," Holmes replied. "Suffice to say that I will let you go. However, if I ever suspect that you have fallen short of the law again, I will swiftly bring you to justice."

The young man's face brightened, as did the young lady's, whom, I might add, I had been gazing at intensely. But she continued to avoid my gaze.

"Just two things," said Holmes, rising and going over to the bell pull and pulling it. "Firstly, I will keep your revolver, and secondly," he paused. I could hear the steps of Mrs. Hudson on the stairs. In a moment, she came in. "Yes, Mr. Holmes?"

"This young man here accidentally broke our window. He'd like to talk with you about having it repaired if you'd take him downstairs."

"Oh, yes, Mr. Holmes. This way, sir."

Ray turned as they were going out. "Thank you, Mr. Holmes, and you, Dr. Watson."

The lady turned also. "Thank you, Mr. Holmes," she paused, and said to me, with slightly lower head and eyes that did not meet mine, "Thank you, sir. I'm sorry."

And they went out.

I stood for a moment in silence. The emotions that had been passing through my brain were leaving me in a state of mild shock.

"Well, Watson," said Holmes, "surely you'll want to know how I deduced this affair? "

He sat down in his chair, fingering the envelope in his hands. I looked at him, and he gave me the glance of a friend who wanted to get his companion's mind off painful thoughts.

"Yes, yes," I said, my mind coming back to its curious nature.

"I must apologize, Watson, for not telling you all I had known during breakfast. I might have spared you some anguish. However, just as I was about to, that untimely message arrived."

My thoughts turned, from the feeling that I had been used and the deep depression I felt, to a desire to find out the why and wherefore.

"Yes, please tell, Holmes.'"

"It was quite simple; once we had arrived at Miss Ray's, or I should say, Mrs. Ray's flat. I sincerely wish that all my opponents left so many clues behind them. The first was the blood, Watson. You observed the broken bottle and the shattered glass, but you did not see that some of the glass-covered spots of blood, indicating that the glass had been broken after, or at the same time, the blood was spilled. This, of course, puzzled me. There were no tracks away from the blood. Obviously, anyone struggling with an assailant who is viciously attacking with a broken bottle would be somewhat hard put as to not step in his or her own blood.

"There were also numerous other points. First, everything was thrown about all over the sitting room and the bedroom. Surely, Watson, if a struggle had occurred, a battle in which one opponent was a member of the gentler sex, why would it have taken two rooms to complete it?

"Second, an examination of the floors of both rooms showed cigar ashes, an abundance of which could only have been built up by a prolonged stay. I doubted that the young lady or her mother smoked cigars.

"Third, the bed showed the indentations of two people sleeping in it, one most likely a man by the deeper impression. There was, of course, the possibility that the young lady was tied or drugged.

"However, the fourth clue; the blue-flowered dress you mentioned the young lady was wearing was not in the apartment, and there were no extra pairs of shoes.

"Fifth, the blood was freshly spilled, as it was still barely wet. If the incident had just occurred before you arrived, I feel the young lady would have been differently attired than she was the previous day. But those clothes were missing, as were any dresses that she might have worn to the theater. There was an absence of any real wardrobe and an absence of any luggage. It seemed to me that it was quite possible that the young lady did not live there and had left of her own free will. The question is, why?"

"You say it was possible? " I asked.

"Yes, Watson, So I went on the chance that if it had been a staging, the woman who played the mother might have been hired to facilitate your meeting the young lady. I went out, and in three hours I had found her. The mole on her ear helped greatly. She stated that a couple had approached her and asked her if she would play a joke on an old friend of theirs for ten pounds. She agreed. An actress by profession, she had been seeing hard times."

"How did you know what they wanted?"

"Simple, Watson. They wanted you to think that she had been abducted. Obviously, they knew you were my colleague. They wanted something in my possession and had staged an act of violence to get it. That was important, Watson, for if they had really done violence, I would never have been able to guess what they were after. By committing no real crime, they gave me a clue. They wanted something that I could not report missing or have any means to bring them to justice for. That was, Watson, this envelope of Dr. Casselman's."

"Who is this, Dr. Casselman?" I queried.

"A sinister fellow who plotted to obtain a high ranking office and sell our country's secrets. As it turned out, his wife was a good English woman who contacted me and asked me to prevent her husband from doing this deed. I would take the papers and instruct him that I would hold them, and, if he attempted the office, I would turn them into the authorities."

"Why did you not turn them in immediately?"

"Surely, Watson, you must realize that such an action would bring scandal upon the man and his wife, and though he was deserving, she was a loyal English woman. She proved that by coming to me. I promised her that I would not turn the papers over as long as her husband did not attempt public office. He, of course, was furious, not knowing how I came about the papers. Now his wife is dead, and the office is again available."

"I understand. Has he tried to get them before?"

"It would have done him no good, Watson. He missed the chance for that office, which is only appointed every two years. He is a cunning man, and he waited six years that I might be off my guard. The position is coming up in a few months, so he is trying to re-obtain the papers."

"But, Holmes, couldn't you still go to the authorities and tell them of his plans? Even if he got the papers back?"

"No, Watson. The most important papers are in his own hand. Without them, I would have no proof, and Casselman would sue me for slander. He surely would win a civil suit and get the appointment the next time it was available.

"He would then merely have to be more careful about his nefarious plans. I would have quite a time getting proof against him, for he wouldn't make the same mistake twice, and, if I got too close, I have no doubt that he would try to eliminate me.

"When the rock came through the window, I saw the young man disappear behind the alley. I saw him peeking around the corner as I left the flat. So I waited around a far corner watching. I did not have to wait that long until a coach appeared, one I imagine he had waiting for him and pulled up in front of our flat. The young man got out and went inside. I waited a minute and then came back. I found the young lady in the cab and brought her up with me."

"Amazing, Holmes."

"You know, Watson, although I like my cases to have a more complicated sheen, this case has given me a great deal of satisfaction."

This statement took me somewhat aback. "How is that, Holmes? Surely you don't derive pleasure in my humiliation?"

"No, Watson. I have nothing but remorse for your hurt feelings. I was thinking of that young couple. You should be well aware of the horrors of crime, of the unholy force it has in our society. Here, Watson, we have been able to pluck the seed before it could grow in the hearts of these two young people. I believe sincerely that we have taught them to think twice before they venture into the shadows of crime."

"Yes, I suppose so," I said, feeling better now that I saw it in that light. "Do you think they'll make out?"

"Yes, Watson. They're young, and they've learned their lesson."

Holmes stood up. "Come, Watson. We have work to do. These letters have to be turned over to the authorities, and then I think I will treat you to the theater."

-The End-

The Adventure of the Monstrous Medium

I had not seen my friend and former fellow lodger Sherlock Holmes in some months since my marriage. My practice was thriving, and, in fact, I had been quite busy. But my wife, Mary, had decided to take a fortnight trip to visit a beloved cousin in Shropshire she had not seen in some time. She was wont to allow me to idle the time at our home alone. She also thought, and I could not disagree with her on the subject, that I had been working rather long hours and needed a break. So, she suggested, why not, while she was visiting her cousin, I should pay a call on Sherlock.

His reply to my post was a pithy "The sooner, the better, Watson!" And the arrangement was set.

I thought I might try to surprise my friend and had the hansom I caught at the train station drop me a short distance from 221 Baker Street. It was an early April day, and the rain had drummed on the roof of my cab, on the way. As I walked to the door of my former lodgings, the sun heated the wet stones so that the street seemed to steam, Rather than knock I used the key still in my possession and found my former landlady, Mrs. Hudson, about to scream in terror at the unexpected breach of the door. But with a finger to my lips and a smile, I was able to allay her fright and was awarded a raised eyebrow as she quickly guessed the purpose of my stealthy entrance. As I made my way to the stairs, Mrs. Hudson coughed slightly and pointed to my shoes. She was right. I removed my shoes and made my way as quietly as I could up the stairs to my former rooms.

The door itself to the apartment was closed, but I assumed not locked. Oh, so gently did I turn the knob and managed to open it quite soundlessly. Once the door was open, I could hear the pluck of violin strings. Holmes was tuning his violin in the main room, most likely by the window where he could not see me. I smiled and began tiptoeing to the central doorway, considering what cry I might utter to render my surprise.

I slipped into the main room and was just about to spring when a butterfly net came down about my head, and I cried aghast.

"Caught you, Watson," Holmes said. He had somehow gotten behind me in the small hallway and hidden in the water closet and was now chuckling to himself. Leaving me to remove the butterfly net, which, I suspected, had been that scoundrel Stapleton's.

When I had managed to free myself from the net, I saw a pendulum-like device hovering over his violin. And realized he had used that to trick me. He, himself, stood by the bay window watching something with field glasses.

"Take a look, Watson. Tell me what you see." Said Holmes handing me the glasses.

Focusing the lenses, the only thing in view was a couple walking side by side away from us. "I see a couple, and that's all."

"Precisely, and what can you tell me about the couple?"

"Very little. Aside from the fact that they know each other."

"How well? Are they brother and sister? A married couple, lovers?"

I watched the two for a few moments more. They walked very closely together, almost in rhythm. "I'd say a married couple," I ventured.

"Good, Watson good. Wrong, but good." He smiled at my frown. "You observed they are intimate and concluded they are married. People in intimate relationships, such as married, walk differently together than others. Their bodies, our bodies speak in a language of their own. I am in the process of doing a monograph on the subject I'm entitling bodily communications."

"But how can you tell these two are not married?"

"Ah, the dress of each. The young woman is dressed rather stylishly in clothing that could not be afforded by the average working woman. No, she is the daughter of some successful merchant or broker. The young man, on the other hand, 's clothing is a bit more threadbare. He has a menial job, and the young woman is above his station. It is not likely her family would approve such a union, so they are, in fact, lovers."

I was skeptical about whether Holmes was right or not. But without actually confronting the couple, there was no way to confirm his views. "But how did you surprise me?" I asked.

Holmes smiled. "For one thing, your Mary sent me a telegram this morning that arrived before you. Thanking me for caring for you in her absence and asking me to remind you of a potion you promised to procure and send to her cousin."

"Humph!" I said. "I did, in fact, remember it and had it sent before I arrived here." I paused a moment considering.

"So you knew I'd arrive today, but you could not have known when."

"I confess," Holmes said, "To looking forward to your visit. So much so I left the door to these rooms ajar at the top of the staircase. When the outer door was opened without a sound, the air stirring in the stairwell caused its hinges to creak. After I assured myself it was you by peeking, I set my violin player to strike a few strings, then snuck into the water closet and waited to surprise you.

"Violin player, humph! It plays so much better than you I should have been alerted," I saw in his eyes my gibe had hit home. "It's so simple when you explain it," I admitted. But promised myself I would succeed in surprising Holmes at some future date.

We spent a few hours reminiscing about old times, speaking of my practice, Mary, and his recent cases over brandy and cigars until Holmes lifted an ear and said, "If I'm not mistaken, there is a carriage outside stopping here."

We both went to the window to see a fine carriage stopped by the front of the house. From the dress of the driver, I could tell the owner of that carriage was quite wealthy.

A moment later, Mrs. Hudson knocked at the door. "Come in," Holmes called. A tall, distinguished-looking man in expensive clothing, with a full head of black hair and dark piercing eyes, entered as Mrs. Hudson held the door for him.

"Lord Ashberry," Holmes said, acknowledging the man, who nodded. "Thank you, Mrs. Hudson, you may leave us."

Mrs. Hudson nodded and backed out the door, shutting it behind her.

The man's eyes moved toward me. I could tell by a slight trembling in his hands that he was highly agitated.

"I'm sure you are familiar with my colleague Dr. Watson. Feels free to speak in front of him as you would in front of me."

Ashberry eyed me unkindly. "I am not," he said, "sure that I want what I wish to speak to you about to be bandied in the Strand Magazine."

"Very many of our cases never see the public eye," Holmes said assuringly. Watson uses the utmost discretion in choosing what he writes about. But I assure you he is invaluable to me in solving our cases."

Ashberry considered this for a time then nodded. "The matter concerns an attempt to extort money from my wife or me via my son, or rather my adopted son, Joseph. He is the oldest of my second wife, Anne, whom she bore in her previous marriage. Both of our previous spouses are deceased. The boy's surname is Parker."

Holmes nodded.

"The boy, or rather I should say young man vanished over a month ago. It is not the first time he has gone his own way for a period. He is 20, undisciplined, and due to his mother, spoiled with a considerable allowance that comes from the estate of his late father.

"About two months ago, at my insistence, albeit reluctantly, my wife reduced his allowance to a pittance. Or what the young man considered a pittance compared to what it was."

I looked at Holmes. Normally he dismissed cases of missing persons offhand as beneath him. But I found Holmes eyeing Lord Ashberry carefully.

"A week ago, my wife received a message from a spiritualist named Madame Rema. This message assured my wife that this person, Rema, had a message from her son. My wife did not inform me of this message right away but rather went to the apartments of this woman without my knowledge."

At that, the man seemed to lose his composure.

"Watson, please pour some brandy for our guest."

I did so and poured the man a stiff dose. He swallowed it quickly.

"When my wife arrived home from the meeting, she was hysterical. This Madame Rema told my wife that the spirit of our son had contacted her. And that he had an important message for her." Lord Ashberry turned to me and looked down toward the bottle still in my hand.

I went forward and refilled his glass. He drank some and held the still partly full glass.

"What was the message," Holmes asked.

"I don't know," Lord Ashberry said crestfallen. "When she told me she had received the note and had gone to see the woman, I reacted badly. I suspected the woman of fraud and deception. I demanded to know how much she had paid the woman before I asked anything else. She accused me of being more interested in money than her son and has refused to speak to me on the matter."

"So, you have no idea how financially involved your wife is with this matter?" Holmes asked.

"Yes, I do," Lord Ashberry said. "I asked her banker. My wife had just withdrawn five hundred pound notes. When I examined her bag, there were four notes left.

So I assume she'd paid this woman £100." For a moment, there was an awkward pause. Then Ashberry reached into his pocket. "I have a photograph of him," Ashberry said, producing a small panel from his pocket. The lad was handsome, light-haired, and bore a roguish grin. He looked, of course, nothing like Ashberry, and I assumed he resembled his parents. But there was something in the way Ashberry handled the photograph that strongly suggested he had feelings for the young man.

"Let us look into this Madame Rema for you. And look into the location of your son. I will get back to you when I know more," Holmes said to my surprise.

"Good. Then I may assume we are done here?" Ashberry said. "Yes," Holmes said. "May we keep the photograph?" Ashberry, nodded, seemingly with reluctance, then turned and walked out.

As I turned to look at Holmes, he was smiling. "You're surprised I agreed to look into this matter, Watson?"

"A little, perhaps, although the man did seem deeply disturbed by the matter. More deeply than what on the face of this, it seems just a common bit of fraud, something more easily handled by Scotland Yard. For a man as influential as Ashberry, they'd surely set this Madame Rema straight."

Holmes jumped from his chair. "But you did notice how upset he was! On the face of it, despite Ashberry's pretending his main interest is in what this may be costing him or his wife, there is something more subtle going on here. Ashberry wore a silk handkerchief in his sleeve. His clothes were freshly laundered. There was a woman's touch in his overall presentation, a woman who cares about him. Love Watson, that is the key. Ashberry could burn £100 a day and not feel the sting.

For some reason, the noble among us feel it is a weakness to act based on emotion. Lord Ashberry came here because he cares about both his wife and son. The fact that Anne Ashberry paid this woman £100 means that the woman has a forbidding hold over Ashberry's family. One that the brute force of Scotland Yard might not handle carefully enough to prevent tragedy."

That evening Holmes lit two candles and placed in different positions by the Bay window overlooking the street. "What time will they arrive?" I asked. "I would think we'll be roused not long after dawn," Holmes replied. "So we both should retire early. We'll have a long day tomorrow."

Mrs. Hudson seemed cranky when she knocked at our door at first light. The first of the street urchins was a dusty lad with worn shoes, a floppy, stained shirt, and holes in his knickers. "Squirt," Holmes addressed him, putting some coins in his palm. He then showed Squirt Joseph Parker's photo. Squirt winked at us and left. Holmes showed that same photo to seeming countless others that almost formed a queue up our stairs that morning.

At midday, as the smallest of the creatures who visited us, a boy named Bobby, who was so encased in grime that he, if indeed it were a he, most likely worked with a chimney sweep left, Homes looked across at me. "I believe that is the last of our forces. Now we must address the issue of Madame Rema. I imagine our best position is to visit this spiritualist posing as clients wishing to contact a loved one. Were your Mary available, I would press upon her to help, but since she is not, the two of us must prevail ourselves."

Just then there was a knocking at the door. Mrs. Hudson called out, "Mr. Holmes, you have an important visitor."

The not quiet exit of Bobby had covered the sound of the entry of another visitor. Holmes looked surprised. Mrs. Hudson had not announced any of the Baker Street Irregulars who simply came up. "Come in," I said.

It was a sharp turn toward the door from the position of my chair, so I was watching Holmes rather than the door as it opened. I could swear that Holmes's jaw dropped, such was the look of astonishment on his face as I rose from my chair and turned.

"Lady Ashberry," Holmes said, rising and going to the woman. She was an astonishing creature, stately, with light hair and a regal look about her. She wore a dark coat and dress. Holmes took her hand and kissed it.

He regarded her with an unreadable expression. "How may I be of service?"

"You need not pretend, sir, that you have no knowledge at all of our family's problem," she said with great dignity. From the sleeve of a black lace glove, she removed a folded scrap of paper. This she handed to Holmes as she added, "I am wealthy in my own right, and had my husband followed, lest he do something to jeopardize my relationship with Madame Rema. My servant reported that he had come here. I was in the process of deciding what I might do about that when I had a visitor who delivered that."

Holmes now opened the paper and read it quickly. When he looked up, his expression was grave. He passed the paper to me as he asked, "This was delivered this morning?"

"Yes."

"By whom?"

"A young girl who looked old beyond her years. She said very little. The butler tried to get her to give him the note, but she insisted she must see me. Her reddish hair was frizzy, and she had a blackened eye. She handed me the note and having no idea who had sent it; I gave her a shilling. I thought she'd left, but I was very relieved she was still there when I finished reading the note. She asked if I wanted to send a reply."

"Did you," Holmes asked, excitedly.

"The fact the note was from Joseph overwhelmed me. I had thought him dead. So I grabbed her by the wrist and demanded to know where she had gotten it. I actually squeezed so hard she cried out in pain. 'I can't tell you, ma'am,' was her reply. It was almost a plea. I let go of her. I told her I'd give her a gold sovereign if she told me where she had gotten the note. She said, 'If I were to take 'at ma'am, I'd not be trusted.' I did not know what to do. She looked so miserable, forlorn, and frightened, but she had character. So I told her I did not have what was requested on hand and would give her a crown if she comes back this evening at 7 for a reply. 'At ood be fine ma'am.' and she hurried off. It was auspicious that Lord Ashberry had come here. I am aware of your reputation but would not have thought of you otherwise. I came right here."

"I am glad that you did. Watson, the note, please." He spread the paper out on the breakfast table."

Mother, Do not fret. I am well. I do find myself, however, in a bit of inconvenience that some funds would remedy. Can you send what you can via young Tally? I trust her and trust you will amply reward her.

Your loving son,

Joseph

"This is your son's handwriting?" Homes asked.

"Yes. I'd know it anywhere," Lady Ashberry replied. Until this moment, she had held herself together. But here I began to see emotion breaking through her control.

"This evening, when the girl returns, you will give her a packet of pound notes. Nothing larger than a pound but enough to provide the package with some weight. Watson and I will be waiting to follow her.

"Do you have another meeting with Madame Rema scheduled?"

"I had a meeting set up for this evening." Anger flared in Lady Ashberry's eyes. "I am going to Scotland Yard after I leave here. The woman led me to believe my son was dead, and she was in communication with his spirit. She defrauded me of a great deal of money, and I aim to see her punished."

"You must do no such thing, Lady Ashberry," Holmes spoke sternly. "Not until Watson and I locate and return Joseph to you."

Lady Ashberry looked taken aback. I imagine she was not used to being spoken to so sternly, even by Lord Ashberry.

"Your son's life may depend on it. I don't imagine you are so easily duped. This woman obviously must have appeared to know things about your son only you and he would know.'

"Yes, and I don't know how she knew them. But if he is alive…"

"That means these people have your son or have access to him. There is no other way they could know intimate details about his situation."

Holmes thought for a moment. "You must keep your appointment with Madame Rema. What time is it?"

"Half-past seven."

Holmes frowned. He paced back and forth in front of the dining table a few times then turned to me. "I will follow the girl. I know the lower quarters of the city better and can do so in disguise. You will accompany Lady Ashberry to Madame Rema's."

I nodded.

"Lady Ashberry, Watson will meet you at your home at quarter past 7 this evening." He turned to me, "We don't want your arrival to frighten the girl."

I nodded my understanding.

"I will be waiting before that to observe and follow the girl. Is that clear?"

"Yes, Mr. Holmes."

"And Lady Ashberry," Holmes continued.

"Yes?"

"I will not tell you what to do, but please consider sharing our plans with Lord Asbury. There are too many things that could go wrong should he decide to interfere."

Lady Ashberry gave him a stern look. "I will consider it," she said.

I showed her out.

"Watson," Holmes said when I returned to the parlor. "These, I believe, are dire circumstances which are far more sinister than they may appear."

Holmes left later that afternoon. He had arranged for a handsome to pick me up at half-past six. The plan was for it to wait across the street from the Ashberry's London flat so that I might see what the girl looked like should it be necessary for me to know later on. I would then be left at the Ashberry's to ride with Lady Ashberry to Madame Rema's.

At 6:30 sharp, Mrs. Hudson knocked on the door. "There's a carriage here for you, Doctor," she said when I opened the door. "And I hope you'll be leaving soon the driver is an appalling man." Without describing the reason for this pronunciation, she left. I was ready. I double-checked the Webley's No. 2 in the front pocket of my long coat with a reassuring pat.

"Good evening to you, Doctor," the driver said in a deep Irish brogue from atop his 4-wheel carriage. He was a scruffy, bent over sort with an old leather eye-patch over his left eye and a few days' growth of beard. Wispy grey hair flew every which way from his cap-less head. Of course, Holmes had ordered a growler rather than a hansom, as the idea was to remain hidden outside the Ashberry's, and I could more easily stay unseen inside the four-person carriage.

"You know where I'm going?" I asked.

"Mr. Holmes was very exact with your honor, so's I knows where we 'r going and what we are to do."

Our trip through the streets was brief enough. We pulled up alongside a row of very expensive flats. "That be the one you want, second down on the far side," the man said, then lapsed into silence. Shortly his snoring told me the lazy drone was asleep. I watched the doorway to the Ashberry's flat from the growler. The street at this time was not busy save for servants going to and fro on errands. There was a sleepy laziness in the air that soon put me into its spell. I may have, in fact, dozed off but for a sudden coughing fit from the driver.

Startled, I soon drew my wits about me and glanced out to see a young woman who looked to be about twelve years of age with flaming red hair approach the door of the Ashberry's flat. At her knock Lady Ashberry, herself appeared. Their transaction took mere seconds. Lady Ashberry offered a package with one hand and placed something in the girl's free hand after she'd accepted the package. The girl nodded, turned, and walked away from the door. Lady Ashberry watched the girl for a moment, then closed the door. The girl must have heard the door shutting for she froze, then turned in a slow circle and took in everything about her. I sat back in the carriage as her eyes swept over it, but she did not see me in the shadow and showed no alarm. She must have been satisfied that there were no watches as she soon proceeded on. I wondered from where Holmes was watching, though I had no doubt he was adequately hidden. I had no idea which direction the girl would take. Still, as luck would have it, she proceeded away from the Ashberry's in the direction of my hansom on the opposite side of the street. Thus I was able to get a closer look at her as she passed.

Unlike the children who resided in Baker Street, the offspring of our neighbors, this girl was gaunt. There was a red bruise on the right side of her forehead. Her arms were thin, and her blue dress with white flowers was threadbare. I was tempted to lean over and gather a better glimpse of her as she passed but resisted to a good result. For suddenly, she stopped broadside to my growler and stared. I found myself holding my breath. But again, she apparently found nothing amiss and continued on. I fought the urge to go to the window and look after her. For if she caught me, it would plainly inform her she was being observed.

"You can relax, Watson," the voice of my colleague rang out above me. "The girl has turned around the corner and is no longer in sight."

I jumped to the door and threw it open and looked up at the driver, who now smiled at me broadly. "Holmes?"

"It is pleasing to know that I can still fool both you and Mrs. Hudson with my disguises. But I must be after that young girl before she gets out of sight." And with that, he leaped from the carriage and rushed past me to the corner before I could utter a word.

As he vanished around the corner, I assume the girl had gone round, I shut the door of the growler. I assumed he had arranged for someone to pick the growler up and walked to the entrance of the Ashberry's flat.

Lady Ashberry's private hansom stopped in front of Madam Rema's. It was a private home on the outskirts of London. We drove up a cobblestone drive, rounded a large and luxurious flower garden, and stopped in front of two large oak doors. The lavishness was far from what I expected. Upkeep alone for such a house would require deep pockets. Lady Ashberry's driver had barely alighted and opened the door of the hansom for us when the front doors opened. Madame Rema was dressed in dark violet and wore a heavy veil.

"Welcome," she said. Then caught sight of me. For a moment, the woman seemed taken aback. Then caught herself. "And who is this?"

Before either Lady Ashberry or I could speak, Madame Rema held a hand up to silence us. For a few long moments, she looked me square in the eye. "Dr. Watson, I believe."

Now it was my turn to show surprise. "My cousin," Lady Ashberry said. "And a somewhat famous one at that. Though few know we are relatives," she added so quickly I almost believed it.

I could not read the expression on Madame Rema's face. But a swirl of questions occupied my mind. How did Rema know me? Because of my published stories about Sherlock's exploits, I was somewhat well known.

The fact that Lady Ashberry had been astute enough to keep up our ruse was commendable. But I had to wonder if Rema would be, now, on the alert. I could only hope that Holmes was successful in following the girl to Joseph Parker, and could recover him successfully.

"Well, all the others are already here," Rema said. "Won't you come in."?

We were led through the lobby and down a bare hallway. Madame Rema threw open a door into a large, red-velvet hung chamber. It was large enough to fit an enormous round table of ebony-colored wood, around which sat nine people in dark, plush chairs. Gas lamps along the wall and five candles on the table itself illuminated the room but only dimly. The occupants of the room were all dressed elegantly and nodded to Lady Ashberry with deference. I took it that she was the only member of the aristocracy in attendance.

"We are starting late," Madame Rema said to me. "I'd introduce you otherwise, but time is pressing for some of my guests, and I think it best that we start immediately. With that, she proceeded to sit in a high-backed chair, which presumably marked the head of the table.

With Madame Rema, there were twelve seated around the table. Lady Ashberry sat to Madame Rema's right and I on Lady Ashberry's right. To my right was a rotund woman with short white hair, diamond earrings, and bejeweled fingers who smiled at me but did not introduce herself. I noticed that the candles, made of black wax, where arranged on the points of a five-pointed star carved into the wood of the table.

Madame Rema took a thin, jewel-encrusted dagger from the folds of her dress and moved it about in front of her. "Only benevolent spirits are welcome here. All others must depart or feel the wrath of my blade."

Watching the others at the time, I realized it this must be something Madame Rema did at every séance.

"It is time to join hands," Madame Rema said. Lady Ashberry took my left hand, and the woman on my right took my right. "Whatever you do," Madame Rema said, looking at me, "Do not let go of the hands holding yours. I could cost me my life." She seemed to be staring at me, so I nodded. This seemed to satisfy her.

"Oh, spirits, we enjoin you to be with us tonight," Madame Rema cried. As she did so, the gaslights dimmed. "If there is a spirit with us who wishes to communicate something to someone present, please make yourself known."

Silence but for the breathing of the group hung in the air held until a gasp issued from someone on the far side of the table. A gust of air scented like the ocean came in from somewhere, extinguishing all the candles at once. In the air, above the center of the table, a mist appeared. Somehow this mist glowed with a faint light. The gas lamps dimmed further.

Lady Ashberry leaned close to me. "Take care not to move your legs about..." she was going to say more, but then there was a loud ringing of bells, the type used on horse-drawn sleighs.

One of the women on the far side of the table gasped. The bells continued for almost a minute. Then there was a sound of something falling like a sack into the snow. The woman, whom I later learned was Mrs. Vault, cried out. Andrew, Is that you?

A profound silence hung in the room—wholly darkened except for the floating, glowing mist. Then the mist seemed to descend toward Madame Rema. For a moment, the mist hovered about Madame Rema's face. Then vanished as Rema spoke out in a surprisingly deep voice. "Andrea, I asked you not to disturb my peace again."

"Andrew," the woman cried, "I am so sorry, but your will cannot be found. Can you tell me where you put it?"

There was a long silence. It seemed everyone at the table was holding their breaths. Finally, the voice of Madame Rema boomed again as a deep masculine voice. "The will is with my solicitors, Warwick and Wallace, at 10 Lambeth Road.

"10 Lambeth Road," the woman repeated.

"Please do not disturb me again, Andrea!" the strange voice boomed from Madame Rema.

I have to admit at this time that I was surprised. If Rema was, as Holmes believed a fraud, then how would she know about where the man's will was? I had to wonder if the woman was a confederate of Madame Rema's.

For a few moments, there was darkness and silence. I could sense the tenseness of the people around me. Then there came a loud knocking. There were three sharp raps, then two soft ones. Silence reigned again for a few seconds. Then the raps repeated in the same sequence: three sharp raps, then two soft ones. All of our hands and forearms were together over the table. Suddenly the table moved and began to rise. The raps repeated now, faster and more intense. I could feel them in the table. It moved about for a moment them seemed to settle down.

"Moria," Madame Rema cried out in another male-sounding voice.

"Yes, yes, my darling," the woman holding my right hand cried. Her fingers clamped down on my own.

"Why do you cling to that old house?"

The woman stammered for a few moments, then, said, in a rather timid manner, "Well, it is, was our home. Where am I to go?"

"To your parents," the voice cried out.

"But what of the house?" she asked.

"Sell it. Sell it as soon as you can to whomever you can. It is an albatross about your neck. I can see someone coming to you very soon to make an offer. Take it and be with your parents. You'll be happier there. Douglas misses you. And your mother does too. She stares out the window on Sundays wishing she could see you walking up the road."

Suddenly, Madame Rema seemed to collapse. Her head sunk to the table. Somewhere off to the side, a voice called, "Madame has collapsed. Turn up the lamps." In moments servants had turned the gas lamps back on. The woman on my right released my hand, as did Lady Ashberry.

"Is that it?" I asked.

"It would seem," Lady Ashberry said. "Sometimes, these sessions exhaust her. When she collapses, the séance is done."

"But, she never spoke to you of Joseph!"

"So I will not be charged for this evening. It is just the way it happens sometimes." At the moment, the woman who had been sitting next to me, and to whom a spirit had just spoken to, was rising from her chair. "Mrs. Moria Pearl," Lady Ashberry said, "I'd like to present you to my cousin. Dr. John Watson."

Mrs. Pearl smiled. "It is nice to make your acquaintance, but I really have to leave, this has been a trial for me."

The woman looked truly shaken, and we nodded as she passed us by and left the room.

Outside when we were well clear of the rest of the guests, I whispered to Lady Ashberry, "The woman whose husband Andrew did not seem pleased to be disturbed. Could she be a plant? Someone in Madame Rema's employ to give her credibility?"

"I don't think so," Lady Ashberry said. "I would be shocked.

"She's Mrs. Vault. Her husband Andrew died while they were on a Christmas hayride. He had a convulsion, stood in the sleigh, and fell off into the snow. The entire account was reported in the newspaper."

I thought for a moment then asked, "Are you certain that the woman who claims to be Mrs. Vault. Is, in fact, that very same woman?"

"Oh, yes," Lady Ashberry said. "My friend Lady Thornbow, who is not here tonight but does come often, knew Mrs. Vault personally before her husband died. Their husbands had done business together."

When I returned to Baker Street, I found Holmes brooding in his chair. A thick cloud of smoke from his pipe hung above him. "I had no luck Watson, in fact, the opposite," Holmes said.

"Did the girl realize you were following her?" I asked.

"I don't think so. In fact, I'm pretty sure she did not."

"But you lost her?"

"This time. But, perhaps there will be another. I left a note for Lady Ashberry with instructions should the girl contact her again."

I looked at Holmes, but he barely returned my glance. Finally, I could take no more. "How did you lose her, on Preston Street no less?"

"There is a wall of mid-level flats running for some distance with no turn in sight. I hung back so as not to be noticed as much as I dared when she seemed to enter a stairway down to a lower level door. I waited a while to make sure it was not just a ruse and that she would not pop out to ascertain if she were indeed followed, but she did not reappear. I hoped I had found her destination. But that, unfortunately, was not the case."

I looked at him, puzzled.

"She had not descended a stairway at all. It was a small, well, leading to a drainage pipe that ran under the building to the far side. As I peeked in, I caught a glimpse of her exiting on the far side. I ducked away quickly lest she see me. However, the pipe was far too small for me to venture through. And I knew I would find no sign of her if I were to traverse around the buildings. No, the only thing to do is to hope we can send her on this same errand again. That she will use this clever ruse to avoid being followed, and that I will be waiting on the other side to continue the pursuit. But tell me of your visit to Madame Rema?"

I explained to Holmes in as much detail as I could what had occurred. He thought for a moment. Then said, "A bad business."

"But how could they possibly know that Andrew Vault's will was in the possession of a solicitor on Lambeth Street?" I asked.

To my surprise, Holmes laughed. "Is it my dear friend?"

He watched the surprise spread across my face. "These are unscrupulous people. The will is missing. Perhaps Andrew Vault died without one. But he had property, which I am sure Madame Rema and her cohorts have checked on extensively. They may or may not have guessed that Mrs. Vault would ask about the location of the will. But they are quick on their feet. The solicitor mentioned is an unsavory one. I am sure by the time Mrs. Vault visits him, a will will be forged that somehow benefits Madame Rema in some way most likely under another name."

"Unbelievable, Holmes."

"I can guarantee it is true," Holmes assured me.

"No, I believe you, it is unbelievable how evil this Madame Rema seems to be."

Holmes nodded. "So what," he asked, "in light of my theory on the nature of Mrs. Vault's spiritual guidance, do you make of the nature of the guidance suggested to Mrs. Pearl?"

I thought for a moment, my mind searching for dark motives. "I've got it," I said. "They will send someone to her shortly to make an offer for her home. It will be way below the actual value, and the poor woman will be afraid not to take it." I offered.

Excellent, Watson. I see your education into the darker side of the world is taking hold."

Then Holmes asked, "When is Lady Ashberry planning on revisiting Madame Rema?"

"Tomorrow night," I said.

"I think perhaps I should go with her tomorrow," Holmes said.

"So, I will not be going?"

"You may if you want to," Holmes replied.

Nothing more was said about the case, and we retired for the evening. A message sent by Lady Ashberry the next morning put a change to our plans.

"The young girl came to Lady Ashberry again with another demand for money," Holmes said, waving the note in his hand. "This changes our plan."

Holmes thought for a moment then looked at me. "Do you think you could undertake to follow the girl?"

I felt almost insulted. "I am pretty sure I am capable of following a small girl around."

"It may be more difficult than you expect. And you should bring your revolver with you."

Holmes situated me on a corner near the exit to the tunnel. I was given an old threadbare coat. Charcoal was smeared across my face. Then some gin, along with some chemical mix of Holmes' design, was splashed onto the coat to give me quite a foul, besotted, and offensive odor. Holmes' last words to me were, "You have your pistol?"

I had nodded my assent. One of his instructions was to speak as little as possible, and I knew he would scold me if I did not stick to that instruction.

"Good," Holmes said. "I hope you do not need it. If you sense any danger, I warn you, I want you to cease pursuit of the girl, noting, of course, your location at the time. Agreed?"

Again, I nodded my assent.

With that, Holmes took off down the street. We had come early so as not to be spied getting into position as it were, by the girl as she made her way to Lady Ashberry's. We could not be confident the girl would come this way coming or going. Still, it was such a sure escape route to avoid being followed Holmes was sure she would use it after she left Lady Ashberry's.

I did not have to wait as long as I thought I might when I saw the girl making her way to the tunnel about a half-hour after Holmes had left. I glanced at her for only a moment. I then produced the bottle of gin Holmes had provided and took a long slug from the bottle, covering my actions with my coat as if I were afraid someone might steal my treasured alcohol away. When I did finally turn in the direction I had seen her, she was gone: most likely through the tunnel, as she was not the sort to live in the houses along the street. I sat back and waited for her return.

Almost a quarter-hour later, I thought I saw movement in the cellar well, but only for a moment. A hansom came rolling down the street, turned, and rushed past me. When I looked again, the girl was up and moving past the edges of the buildings on a street perpendicular to the one where I sat. Quickly, rising, teetering a bit drunkenly to protect my role, I stumbled after her. She was a quick little thing. As I rounded the corner where I last saw her, she was a hundred yards ahead. Had she run? No matter, now she was walking, albeit swiftly. I stumbled along as best I could in as quick a gait as I could muster. My leg wound began to bother me almost immediately. We soon left the better neighborhoods and began to delve into the more impoverished regions of London. The streets became more crowded. Women of the evening, who would have approached me were I dressed normally glanced my way then looked back to their business without interest. Now that others were in the streets, I quickened my pace to get closer to the girl who was no longer hurrying, perhaps because that would draw attention to her here. The vile scents of the street assaulted my nostrils even over the chemicals Holmes had doused me with.

I caught sight of the girl turning a corner up ahead and ran to catch up, least I lose her. As I ran suddenly, a foot stuck out in front of me. I fell, bruising my hands. Cruel laughter rang out overhead. A tall, thin man with a black mustache laughed. Containing my anger, I jumped up and ran on. I had thought I lost her when I caught a glimpse of her in the distance. I hurried and saw her turn into a doorway. I slowed my pace. The doorway had no sign. It was just a dark entryway, which was open. I stepped inside. I stepped into a dark corridor. I heard someone behind me, and then all went dark.

I awoke sometime later. I was in a bed. Something like fog or smoke drifted through the air. A dim light came from lamps on the walls. As I tried to move, I realized that there was an iron shackle on my right arm holding me to the bed. When I tried to move my legs, I discovered there was also an iron shackle on my right leg. Although my left leg and arm were free, there was no moving from the bed. I recognized the scent in the air. Opium. I was in an opium den.

"Aye, your awake?"

I looked up. An unkempt fellow in soiled clothing stood by the bed addressing me.

"What do you want?" I demanded.

"Well, for one thing, fellow, I want to know why," he paused and pulled my Webley from his pocket. "Why you entered my establishment carrying the likes of this?"

I had to think quickly. "That's mine," I said firmly. "I found it on the street this morning. Someone dropping it was my luck. Now you give it back."

He laughed. "Not likely," he sneered, "not likely at all."

"We'll see about that?" I said.

"Let's get down to business, shall we? Why were you following young Tally?"

"Tally?"

"The young lady who entered my fine establishment just before you did?"

What would Holmes do in a case like this? I found myself asking myself. And then an idea came to me. "Tally, no. I was following my young Cassie. Twelve years she be and a handsome young girl. I saw her and followed her. Is she here?"

"Well, no, she not be here right now. And I cannot vouch that her name has never been Cassie. But how long has it been since you last saw her?"

The man was trying to trap me in a lie. I had no idea how long he had known of the waif. If I named a date too soon in the past, he would see through my lie in an instant."

I pretended to strain in thought. "I don't know," I said. "We had a house on Merchant. And then…"

He, or someone working for him, had hit me on the head. As a physician, I knew that strikes to the head could cause memory loss, temporary or permanent. I shook my head. "I can't remember…"

He looked at me for a long time as I feigned forgetfulness. Then a Chinese ran up to him. He leaned down as the man whispered in his ear. He frowned.

"It seems I have another problem. I will be back for you," he said and left with the Chinese.

They had been gone a short time when a voice issued from the bed beside mine to the left. "Are you the father of this young girl?"

In the dim, smoky room, I could barely see into the aisle between the beds, much less to the next bed. "Who is there?" I asked.

"Sorry, this is not the place for introductions. I'll leave you be." A youngish voice said. A voice that obviously had some education.

"Why do you ask," I ventured. "I saw a girl who looked like my lost Cassie and followed her here. Now, I am a prisoner chained to this bed."

"I am chained too," he said, rattling a chain that I could barely make out, that was fastened about his left arm. "I simply asked because the girl, whom I know as Tally, has been of some help to me. But I fear your following her has placed her in some danger from the people who run this place."

"No!" I said, leaning toward him. "What happened?"

"She came to see me. Had a message, she often comes to deliver things to the more wealthy patrons of this fine establishment." I could hear the sarcasm in his voice. "But Murdock, the owner came in shortly after she approached me and dragged her off, asking if she had been so careless as to have been followed. I've been worried about her ever since."

It occurred to me that this must be Joseph, or if not, someone who would know of the young man. But it also occurred to me that if he was not Joseph, and his conversation was, in fact, a deception, revealing the true nature of my task would not benefit the young girl or myself.

"I lost my Cassie. I haven't seen her in some time," I said, and then let an empty pause hang in the air for a bit longer than a normal person would ever do. "I thought I saw her today and followed her here."

Just then, a young Chinese girl came between us and handed the young man a pipe. Without saying another word, he let the pipe be lit and began puffing at the thing. After a time, the young girl took the pipe away, and the young man was silent.

"Are you still there?" I asked. The man in the next bed did not reply.

I must have slept also. When I again awoke, it seemed some time had gone by. The same lamps illuminated the same, dim, poppy-laden air. But I realized I was hungry and that most likely, I had slept through a night. Realizing also that this gave me an excuse to talk to the young man again, I leaned over as far as I could and landed three solid blows to the bed there. The thumps were soft and probably did not carry far, but the figure in the bed beside me stirred. I could not see his features but could make out that he was turning his head about as if confused.

I struck the bed another blow. This time, his attention focused on me.

"Do they feed us here?" I said, trying to sound desperate. "I'm starving, I don't know the last time I've eaten."

"Let me see," the man said.

I saw him moving about. And realized he was procuring a pocket watch from his coat. I wondered what the fact that they had not taken it away from him meant.

"Almost, half 7," he said. "They'll be bringing me my gruel soon. If they've chained you, it is likely they will feed you too. Does your family have money?"

"No," I said. "I mean, I think I had money, but it was lost."

"How odd," he said, after a bit, "I don't know why they'd keep you then."

I saw my chance, and with our current conversation, the question would not seem out of place. "Are you from a moneyed family then?" I asked.

"It's a long story," he said and seemed about to tell it when a Chinese man suddenly appeared between us. He had a cart with two big wheels with a foot-like post in front, much like a wheelbarrow, although he pulled it rather than pushed this cart. He stopped between us. The Chinese looked at me and grabbed my free hand and thrust a bowl into it. Something hot splashed against my palm. The Chinese turned his attention to my companion.

"Eat as quick as you can," the voice from the next bed called, then I watched him take the bowl and lift it to his mouth. I could hear him slurping from the bowl. Not knowing how long I'd be allowed to keep the food, I assumed I should follow his advice and eat to keep my strength up. I tasted the concoction in the bowl. It did not taste bad. I quickly gulped it down and was glad I did when the Chinese turned and grabbed the now-empty bowl away from me.

When the Chinese was gone, I turned my companion. He was lying back and seemed to be thinking.

"You were about to tell me why you are here?" I asked.

He shook his head. "Best, you don't know," he said. "If they find out you know of me, you may not leave here alive."

"It doesn't matter a bean to me boy who you might be, not a bean. I just wanted to find my Cassie," I said indignantly, for some reason, sensing that I needed to stay in character. I was glad that I did. The beds formed long rows along the low-ceilinged room. The young man was across from me, but there was a bed behind my head and another at my feet. As I lay back, a figure jumped up from the bed behind my head and strolled away. I was familiar enough with opium dens to know that this was not the usual physical behavior of an opium addict.

I learned later that Sherlock was not idle. When I had not returned by 10 p.m., he became concerned. He contacted Wiggins, and within hours the entire body of the Baker Street Irregulars were out searching for Tally and myself. Holmes had paid each searcher and offered a reward for the one who found Tally or me. Within hours two of the irregulars, a tall thin lad named Thomas and a little chubby dark-haired fellow, nicknamed, Cheeky, had found Tally together as they scoured the alleys of East London. The girl had been severely beaten and left for dead. Cheeky had gone so far as to spend the small sum Holmes had paid him on broth and a beef pie for the girl, then had tended to her while Thomas had gone to fetch Holmes.

Holmes had rewarded both boys handsomely. But Tally was in a horrible state, and could not or would not speak. Holmes decided to take Tally to Lady Ashberry's. He explained to Lady Ashberry that if she were taken to a hospital, she might just run off. She needed care, but the young girl also required protection. Although at first, Lady Ashberry seemed a bit taken aback at the prospect of keeping a waif from the streets in her home, Holmes reminded her that she was a trusted friend of her son's.

The rest of that day passed for me slowly. A Chinese girl brought a pipe to me, but I brushed her aside. She did not return, nor did the man who had accosted me when I first arrived. I was not fed again, and soon my stomach was growling. Finally, I fell into a fitful sleep.

I awoke to the sound of police whistles, clubs smacking flesh. I heard cries in Chinese, a scream, and saw blue uniforms run down the aisle beside me. Moments later, a dark figure stood beside me in the aisle to my left "I think I've found him, Holmes," I heard the voice of Inspector Lestrade call out loudly above me. He bent down and grinned at me. "Glad to find you alive, Doctor," he said. He then called down the aisle of beds, "Constable Smythe, bring your iron keys over here," He reached down and rattled the chain on my ankle. "We'll have these off in an instant," he added.

Holmes appeared next to him a moment before the constable arrived. "Watson, you gave me a scare, I must say," Holmes said.

"Holmes. Thank God. I think you'll find Joseph Parker in the bed to my right," I said.

Lestrade turned. He leaned over the bed to my left, and I heard him rattle chains there. "There is no one in that bed, now, Doctor. Just empty chains."

It took us a while to actually leave. Holmes and Lestrade had questions for the Chinese workers and patrons, and they wanted to ask them while the workers were still in shock over the police raid. Finally, the last worker had been questioned, and Holmes indicated it was time to leave.

"Don't feel too badly, Watson," Holmes said on the carriage ride back to Baker Street. "You are alive, and we can presume that so is Joseph Parker, at least for now."

I said nothing, as my thoughts were whirling about the missed opportunity to save Joseph Parker.

Holmes interrupted my thoughts. "You think that if we had gotten there sooner, we would have saved him too?"

"Yes, those were my thoughts," I replied, honestly.

"Perhaps," Holmes said, "or perhaps you both would have met a darker fate."

Holmes explained then how Tally had come around after just one evening with Lady Ashberry. Tally revealed where both you and Joseph were being held. I must say Lady Ashberry has become quite taken with the young girl."

"But you didn't find Joseph Parker," I said. "And now it seems we are back at the beginning."

"Not at all Watson, we now know from Murdock's Chinese workers, who were loath to meet the hangman, that Madame Rema's relative, Murdock, kept Joseph a prisoner for her in his opium den. The police are scouring the streets for him now. Joseph was a frequenter of Murdock's establishment. When Murdock realized that the boy had money, he arranged for Joseph to awaken from an opium dream in one of the private rooms with one of the Chinese girls. However, they'd freshly murdered the girl and put the bloody knife in Joseph's hand. They then began to blackmail young Joseph. Yet, Lord Ashberry's having cut off his allowance made it impossible for him to pay blackmail. Murdock, in his own ingenious way, concocted a way to involve his cousin, Madame Rema, in a new scheme to fleece Lady Ashberry, Joseph's mother, of her money. They milked him for private information while he was under the influence of opium, most likely holding the drug back from him unless he provided the information they needed.

"But how will we find Joseph Parker now that Murdock has fled?"

"When the police find Murdock, he'll face the gallows. Revealing the location of Joseph Parker could be a bargaining chip for him. So I doubt he will harm Joseph, at least not yet. Meanwhile, I suspect that Madame Rema will want to make the most of Joseph while she can. And I have a plan."

It was our luck that Lady Ashberry had once aspired to the theatre and had studied acting, as some acting talent was necessary for Holmes's plan to work. The following afternoon, after some convincing on Holmes' part, of both Ashberry and his doctor, Lord Ashberry was reported to have died. This necessitated a very hastily arranged meeting between Lady Ashberry and Madame Rema. One very-cooperative Chinese who had worked at Murdock's assured us that Murdock had no idea who I actually was. The Chinese explained that as the "Duck," as he called Murdock, had been called away so soon after I arrived, he had not actually gotten a good look at me. Having been thus assured, I decided to attend with Lady Ashberry.

Madame Rema herself, escorted us to the séance room. At the large table, Lady Ashberry put on a marvelous characterization of the new widow. Tears, most genuine in nature, poured from her eyes.

"There, there," Madame Rema soothed. "I know of the death of Lord Ashbury. I have seen him."

"You have," Lady Ashberry said, rising from her tears, a note of hope in her voice.

"Yes, I have. He is sorry that he left you without notice. But he seems confused about his own death. If there is anything he can help you with, I will do all I can to help. But your late husband needs a little time to get used to his current state."

Lady Ashberry paused, looked at me, and then back at Madame Rema. I nodded to her as if to agree with her unasked question.

"It is about the will," Lady Ashberry said with almost real distress. "Thurston never told me where he kept it. We've searched and searched. Only he and Joseph knew where it was."

Madame Rema closed her eyes. The room darkened as the gas lights dimmed. The glow I had seen above the table returned. There were three sharp knocks on the table.

"Your husband is here," Madame Rema said.

"Did he hear my question?" Lady Ashberry asked.

"It would be best if you repeat it to him directly," Madame Rema said.

"Thurston," Lady Ashberry cried out with the passion of someone who has just lost a loved one, "Can you tell me where you kept your will?"

We all listened, but the only response was silence. "Only you and Joseph knew where it was?" Lady Ashberry begged.

Again there was silence. After a long silent pause, Lady Ashberry then asked beseechingly, her voice betraying the tears running down her cheek and glistening in the dim light. "Is Joseph there with you?"

There were three loud knocks on the table.

Madame Rema seemed to concentrate. Finally, she spoke. "Thurston is too confused to answer. And

Joseph seems obsessed this evening with an event in his childhood. His father, your first husband, beat him for something he didn't do. Three hard spanks with his right hand to Joseph's bottom. "

"I remember that," Lady Ashberry said. She glanced my way as if to ask how she could know that.

"It had to do with a ball at school. Someone said he stole it."

"He did not steal it," Lady Ashberry said. "The other boy confessed he'd lied. He was the one expelled."

Madame Rema's head fell forward on the table. For a half-minute, she was still, and then she sat up. "I'm sorry, that is all I can do for today. But come back tomorrow, and we will try again." She took Lady Ashberry's hand. "There will be no charge for today. You are my friend, and I want to help you."

Once we had safely boarded Lady Ashberry's carriage and were whisked away, I said, "Help, herself to your fortune, by changing your husband's will,"

"My late husband, no less," Lady Ashberry added, laughing. "It really was all I could do to control myself and keep myself from strangling the woman."

The carriage stopped a block away. "Keep my son safe, Dr. Watson, please," Lady Ashberry begged.

"We will do our best," I promised.

Holmes, Lestrade, and several constables were arranged outside Madame Rema's. Holmes had four of the fastest hansoms in London parked nearby in case we needed to give chase to a carriage. But not long after we arrived, Madame Rema emerged from her home and began strolling down the street on foot.

Obviously, wherever they held, Joseph now was close by. We didn't even need to step out of hiding to follow her. She entered an old brick building just a few doors down.

"Where do you think they are holding Joseph Parker prisoner?" Lestrade asked Holmes.

"I see no lights on the upper floors. There must be a subfloor below. That is my guess where the young man is being held." Holmes said. "But we must be careful. There could be tunnels leading away by which they could make their escape. Leave two constables here to enter after five minutes if they hear gunshots. Meanwhile, you, Watson, and I will work our way to the back and see is there is a cellar door."

There was, in fact, a below-ground door in the back of the house. Brick steps led down to a small cave-like opening in which the entry was set. A grimy glass window in the door showed just flickers of light. "You have a pistol, Watson?"

"Yes," I said, lifting the one Lestrade had lent me. A search of the opium den had not discovered my Webley.

"Let's go," Holmes said.

The cellar door was locked, but Holmes removed a small case from his pocket and made quick work of the lock while Lestrade looked away. Holmes opened the door carefully so as not to make a sound. We found ourselves in a narrow corridor lit by flickering lamps, much like the ones in the opium den. Carefully we made our way down it until about ten yards in we could hear voices in a room up ahead. They were indistinct at first, and then I recognized the voice of Madame Rema.

"You will tell me what I want to know, or you will no longer be a man," she said. The threat in her voice now revealing just how evil this woman really was.

"I tell you I don't know anything about my step-father's will. It was not something he would share with me."

"What if he's telling the truth?" a male voice, I recognized as Murdock's, said.

"I can read my clients. Lady Ashberry was filled with grief. She was not lying."

There was a scream, which I assumed was Joseph Parker's.

Holmes and Lestrade rushed forward and turned the corner ahead. I followed. As I entered the room better lit with four lamps, the tableau opened. Joseph was again chained to a low bed. Madame Rema stood above him her knife bloody, and line of blood running from a cut in Joseph's bare chest. At the sound of our entrance, all glanced toward us. Murdock grabbed a shotgun leaning against the wall and began to swing it in our direction. Lestrade and I fired at the same time. Murdock staggered, back, dropped the gun, and collapsed to the floor. Holmes took the distraction to rush to Madame Rema and grab the hand holding the knife. They struggled, and Holmes wrested the knife away. Rema gave a cry and went for Holmes' eyes, but Lestrade moved in, pressed his revolver to her head, and she ceased her attack. The hatred seethed from her eyes. The constables entered then, guns drawn, and the monstrous medium seemed to collapse in defeat.

"You think she's predicting the gallows for herself, Mr. Holmes?" Lestrade observed as the constables took her away.

I examined Joseph's wound. It was not deep, and the bleeding had almost stopped. "Are you alright to walk?" I asked. "I'll get you to somewhere where I can tend that."

Joseph returned home, and Lady Ashberry was exceedingly grateful, as was Lord Ashberry. Holmes received a cheque from him soon after, which contained a rather substantial sum. We learned that Joseph insisted that Tally become the Ashberry's ward, and both Lord and Lady Ashberry agreed.

Epilogue:

Madame Rema had funds and many influential friends who would not believe she was a fraud. By claiming that Murdock forced her to do what little she did, her crime earned her only 8 months in gaol.

-The End-

The Adventure of the Shanghaied Sailor

As I mentioned earlier in a story entitled "The Adventure of the Monstrous Medium," my wife, Mary, had insisted that I take a holiday from work. At the same time, she visited a favorite cousin in Shropshire. She had suggested that I visit my friend Sherlock Holmes and Holmes quickly agreed.

The visit had indeed been enjoyable so far as we had just solved the case mentioned, in fact, it was just the day after the solving of that case I had decided, after receiving a letter that morning from Mary urging me to do so, to take a day trip to visit a friend on the outskirts of London who was my physician. When I left in the morning, Holmes barely seemed to notice my departure as he sat at the table where he conducted his chemical experiments concentrating on something. Though he did give a slight wave.

When I returned, I was in good spirits. My friend had declared me to be in excellent health and had already sent a telegram to Mary at her cousin's informing her of that fact. When I returned to Baker Street, I met Mrs. Hudson by the door. She had packages in her arms, which I helped her with. For my trouble, I was informed that Holmes had had no visitors up to the time that she went out to shop. While I was lodging with Holmes before my marriage, there were often days when there were no clients. I actually enjoyed the peace on those days. Still, I knew the boredom weighed upon my friend and often led to his indulgence in a seven percent solution of cocaine.

As I reached the doorway to the flat, I wondered if I would find that Holmes had resorted to the needle and prepared myself mentally to give him a firm lecture if he had. But to my astonishment, when I opened the door, billows of smoke bellowed out and rose toward the ceiling.

"Fire," I cried, "Fire!"

I heard Mrs. Hudson below me run into the parlor. "Oh, no!" she cried.

Suddenly Holmes brushed past me emerging like some demon from the clouds of smoke and shouted down the stairway, "Everything is under control, Mrs. Hudson. Just a bit of smoke, but no fire."

I looked down at the woman below us. Her eyes bore into my friend's. Then she shook her head and went back into her flat.

Holmes' eyes found mine. "Do you remember the plumber's smoke-rocket we used in the case involving that woman?"

I looked at him in surprise. "I could hardly forget that. You bring up Irene Adler quite often, you know."

"Well, the smoke-rocket we used produced ample smoke but dispersed all of the smoke rather quickly. I have found by experiment that the addition of a small amount of bicarbonate of soda to the mixture of saltpeter and sugar makes the rocket burn slower and last longer."

"Marvelous," I said skeptically. And entered the flat and made my way through the smoke and opened a window. Holmes, taking the hint, went into his own bedroom and opened a window there.

When he returned, the flat was beginning to air out.

"Something tells me that she is not carrying a message," Holmes said.

I had no idea what he was talking about.

"If she were, I would assume I would have seen her carrying it as she made her way here. She also moved like someone who is in a bit of distress."

It was then that I heard footsteps on the stair. A moment later, there was a knock.

"Come in," Holmes called.

The door opened, and Mrs. Hudson peeked in. "Someone to see you, Mr. Holmes."

"Send her right in, Mrs. Hudson.

"You remember Robin Tell, don't you Watson."

I remembered the woman as the only female driver in our experiments to find the fastest cab drivers in preparation for future needs. She had driven the fastest four-wheeler and was only a shade behind the best time of all, which was for a two-wheeler.

"Mrs. Tell," I said. "Good to see you again. But I gather this isn't a social call."

Holmes gave me a look, which I took to mean I was correct. But the fact that the woman was distressed was evident in the fact that she held her gloves in her hands and was twisting them tightly.

"No, Dr. Watson," she said. She turned to Holmes. "I was hoping you might be able to help me?"

"Sit down, please," Holmes said, indicating a chair. "Watson?"

"Can I offer you some brandy?"

"Yes, please," she said.

"What is the problem?" Holmes asked.

Mrs. Tell took a deep breath. "My son, James, has disappeared."

"How old is your son?" Holmes asked.

"He is twenty this year. He went out the other night to meet a young woman, and he has not returned. And I know young men sometimes don't come home, but this time I fear something has happened to him. I went to the police, but they did not seem that interested in helping me and just told me to go home. They said he'd probably show up sooner or later."

"What makes you think he might not come home?" I asked as I set the brandy before her.

She looked at me and then at Holmes. "It is this woman he went to see. I saw her with him once while I was working. I stopped to talk. There was something about her that just didn't seem right. I could tell the way a woman can, that she was much older than my son. But I mentioned that to him he said I was wrong and she was his age and was angry with me."

"Do you know the woman's name?" Holmes asked.

"Mary Barkley," Mrs. Tell said. "That is if she is telling the truth. She was a pretty thing, tall with golden hair and green eyes. I could see what it was he saw in her, but I don't know what she saw in him. She wore expensive clothing. More expensive than my son could afford."

Holmes nodded. "Do you know where he was going to meet her the night he did not come home?"

"Not exactly. When I asked, he seemed annoyed that I was questioning him. Finally, when I kept asking, begrudgingly, he said 'the docks if you must know."

Suddenly, the woman began to cry. Tears rolled down her face. She picked up the glass I had given her and drained it. "I am so afraid that something terrible has befallen him."

Holmes thought for a moment before answering. "I do not think from what you have told us that your son has been injured in any way. But Watson," he glanced at me, and I nodded my assent, "and I will look into this for you."

"Thank you, Mr. Holmes," she said, then turned to me, "And you too, doctor."

After I had shown her out, I found Holmes puffing on his black briar. "What makes you think the boy is not hurt or worse?"

"I think I know of the woman he was with. I had not heard of her using the name Barkley before, if it is the woman I am thinking of, then Mary Barkley is merely one of her aliases."

"But what would any woman, who dresses well, want with the son of a cab driver. The family has no money. What can they possibly gain?"

"The lad himself is the value. The woman whom I suspect James Tell was seeing is a crimp, and her purpose in seducing young James was to shanghai him."

"But I thought that only happened to sailors in bars who got drunk and were jumped, like that John Fall fellow you located for Miss May Bainbridge?"

"Yes, and though I found out what happened to him, she had to wait until his return from sea. The law is unjust when it comes to shanghaiing. They trick or coerce a man into signing ships papers: the crimp usually receiving as much as three months of the man's wages. In Fall's case, he got drunk, and the papers were probably forged. But this case is different. I would guess that Mary told James she wanted to marry him but not in the Anglican Church. So instead of going through the process of the calling of banns, they would have to get a license for a civil ceremony. She probably got him drunk and told him the ship's papers where the license."

"So, what can we do?" I asked.

"We must find this Mary Barkley and then find out what ship the young man is on."

The next morning when I came down to breakfast, I found six street children, whose clothing was so tattered and whose hair so tangled I could not tell if they were boys or girls, assembled in our sitting room. Holmes had just finished giving them a set of instructions and was now placing a few pence in each of their hands. With a wave, he ushered them out the door, and they vanished like scared mice.

"Ah, Watson," Holmes said. "I trust you slept well?"

"Yes. Yes, I did," I said. "I see you've engaged the irregulars. I presume in pursuit of Mary Barkley."

"Indeed, or a woman who resembles her. The lads I had here this morning live on the streets by the docks, for that is where I think our prey lurks. I only hope they can find a lead before the ship bearing James Tell departs."

I had just arrived back at 221B Baker Street from the tobacconist, where I purchased a fresh supply of my Arcadia mixture when Holmes emerged from the door.

"Just in time, Watson," Holmes cried. We have a location for our crimp, but she has changed her name again."

"Should I fetch my Webley?"

"I don't think to be armed will be necessary. Ah, there is a cab now."

We soon arrived at an establishment called 'The Warm Wench,' which was close enough to the dock that we could smell salt on the air and dead fish. The sign on the door was faded and in need of paint, and the portrait of the wench looked more like a cold ghost than an object of male desire. The interior was so dim we had to stand by the doorway before we could move around without falling over something. The air smelled of vomit, urine, stale beer, and tobacco smoke.

"Can I get ye gents som'en to eat or drink," a voice said from the darkness.

"Yes, indeed, my good man, you may," Holmes said, "But perhaps a seat at a table first."

"That I can do," he said. "The name is Jasper, and I'm the proprietor of this fine establishment," he added as our eyes adjusted to the dimness. We followed his dark form as he led us to a bench before a simple table, and then made a show of dusting the bench off with his apron. Even in the gloom, the table still looked grimy. He bade us sit.

"And what can I bring you?" he asked, "We've got a fresh catch of mullet."

"Just your finest ale for now," Holmes said. "Pints both."

"I'll be right back," Jasper said and vanished across the floor.

"Are you going to ask him about the woman?"

"Not just yet," Holmes said. "He may be her confederate and warn her off. According to my source, she has been here for some time today. Let us see if we can spot her ourselves."

We searched the dim room from our bench. There were women in the room, but none of them had golden hair. When our proprietor came back with our ale, Holmes asked, "Do you have a private room we might use?" He placed a half-crown in the man's hand. "We have some private business to discuss."

"Certainly sir," the man said, pocketing the coin. "It's occupied at the moment, but they is leaving as we speak. Let me just go check on said room's availability."

Our eyes had adjusted to the gloom by then. We watched as Jasper entered a door off to the side of the room. A moment later, he was shouting so loud we could hear his voice but not make out what he was saying. A moment later, two new figures emerged from the room. One was a short man with a black bowler hat and a black Norfolk jacket. A light-haired woman wearing a tailored jacket with a poke bonnet followed this person. Both looked angry as they made their way to the door.

The man walked ahead. As soon as he passed our table, and before the woman did, Holmes stood up. "Mary Barkley, I presume," He said, holding up a hand. The woman stopped and stared at him before saying, "You are mistaken, sir," and moved to step by him. Holmes took her left arm, restraining her. The man at that point turned and said, "See here," loudly and with menace. But Holmes had anticipated such an encounter by someone with the woman and had prepared me in the cab. I held out a five-pound note in my left hand and put my right hand in my pocket, pushing my index finger forward as if it were a gun. "I believe you have an appointment outside," I said.

The man looked at the note, then at the woman and Holmes and me. He then grabbed the note, turned, and walked out the door of the pub. It was then that the proprietor emerged from the back room. He took one look at the situation, shook his head, and walked back to the bar.

The woman watched him go, then turned to Holmes. "What do you want, sir. I am a lady and not used to such ill-handling."

"Information, that is all, Mary," Holmes said calmly.

"What information?" she asked.

"Where did you crimp James Tell," Holmes said.

"I ain't got no idea what you a jabbering about," she said, feigning insult.

"Holmes held up a twenty-pound note," I am willing to pay for the information, my dear, and pay well for the answers to some simple questions."

I could tell by her expression that she was thinking of denying the charge. But the easy money won out.

"Go ahead and ask em," she said, reaching for the note.

Holmes pulled it back. "The name of the ship and when it departs."

"The ship is the Barcelona Swan, she's down by the east dock, and she ships out in the morning day after tomorrow."

"And how did you get the papers signed?"

I could see the woman's hesitation. This was something she did not want to admit, but the money again won out.

"He wanted to marry me, I had him sign a license, but it weren't no license, see."

"Thank you," Holmes said and pushed the money forward and let go of her arm. "I trust it is accurate information. Because we can find you again."

"I'm a lady," she said, "And I don't lie." With that, she turned and left the bar.

The next morning I arrived at the dock alone. I was familiar with the new Blue Riband-class steam-powered liners such as the North German Lloyd Steamship Company's Kaiser Wilhelm der Grosse. But the Barcelona Swan was nothing like that 655-foot testament to progress. The Swan was an old Clipper converted to steam with a large, dirty smokestack toward the back and masts for sail in the front. It was a dark ship that seemed to collect gloom about itself. A grimy dark-looking man in a black wool shirt and cap met me as I stepped onto the gangplank and blocked my passage at midway. "Permission to come aboard?" I asked.

"Whata ye be want'n here?" he asked.

"I have business with the captain," I said.

The man looked me up and down. He had a stubble of a black beard, and his face was like creased leather. He held me with a mean look. "And what business have ye with the Capt'n?"

"That is between me, and he, sir!" I said sternly.

"Well, being that I is the Capt'n, I says you are a liar."

I held my temper. "I never said I met you, sir, just that I have business with you, of a monetary nature."

He gave me a quizzical look that somehow managed to appear a threat.

"Of a nature to your financial advantage," I added.

"Whata you mean my financial advantage?"

It was then I heard a sound of a step behind me. Whether it was a crew member or not, I decided not to turn.

"I am the representative of a Mrs. Tell who wished to buy back the contract of her son, James Tell, who was shanghaied as a crew member of this ship."

Anger flared in the man's eyes. "He ain't no shang-hai," the man barked at me, "He's signed ship papers and dare ain't no way I'm letting him free of 'is con-tract."

"But sir, we are willing to be generous in our pay-ment."

"Get off my plank, or I'll have you thrown in." He gestured toward the dark water.

"You do, and I'll have you arrested, sir," I protested.

"You are on his ship, and he can throw you over-board, you old knut," a voice roared from behind me.

Before I could utter another word, the rogue grabbed me by the back of my collar with one hand, my left arm with the other and flung me around, and sent me off-balance down to the end of the gangplank.

I looked back to see a tall, dark figure of a sailor, as dirty as the captain in a well-worn blue jacket standing in the center of the plank, with the captain laughing behind him so hard he was bent over. Anger flared in my breast. I stormed back, but before I even got close to him, the tall stranger pulled a long knife from his coat and brandished it before me.

Instinctively, my hand went for my revolver. But my hand landed on an empty pocket. I had not brought the gun at Holmes' insistence. I looked the man for a moment, then thought the better of it, and turned and walked away.

I returned to 221B Baker Street and changed into more comfortable clothing. I had just lit my pipe when the door burst open. Who but the sailor who had threatened me on the gangplank of the Barcelona Swan burst into the door. I jumped from my chair, searching for a weapon near at hand when the sailor spoke, but not in the voice he had used on the ship. "Watson, it is I."

"Holmes?" I could not believe it.

With a wave of his hand, he removed dark-eyebrows and his cap. It was Holmes.

I was searching for something to say when Robin Tell entered behind Holmes, followed by a young man.

"Dr. Watson, may I present James Tell," Holmes said.

The resemblance to his mother was strong.

"Pleased to meet you," I said.

"And I am pleased to meet you, Dr. Watson," the young man said. "And I am most grateful to you."

"As am I," Robin Tell added. "I don't know how I will repay the both of you, but if you'll just send me a bill…"

"I think," Holmes said, "That if you just repay us with transportation from time to time…" Holmes glanced at me, and I nodded my approval. "We can call it even."

"Thank you, Mr. Holmes, and Dr. Watson."

With that, mother and son left. When the door shut behind them, I asked. "How did you manage it?"

"Very simply, Watson," Holmes said, extracting his black briar and filling it from his Persian slipper. "After I had persuaded you to leave the ship as I did, the captain was in a friendly persuasion. I told him I was a ship's cook, and he agreed to give my cooking a try, although he had a cook who was ashore. I think the man just wanted a taste of something new. I had brought three of my improved smoke-rockets with me. When I came up from the galley with smoke billowing behind me, shouting 'fire' the sheer volume of smoke persuaded the captain to yell for all hands to abandon ship. And what small crew was on board quickly did."

"But surely," I asked, "if there was no real fire and no damage, didn't they force Tell to go back on the ship?"

"You're not completely correct in saying there was no damage. There was no physical damage to the ship at all." He paused and looked at me.

I gave Holmes a questioning look.

"They brought him up, and he exited the ship with everyone else. There were chain marks upon his wrists as they were keeping him under lock and key least he escape before the ship sailed. Once he was safely ashore, I whisked him away before anyone was the wiser."

"But wouldn't they still have a contract. Can't they come after him?"

"No, my smoke-rockets did irreparable damage to James Tell's contract. Once the captain cried abandon ship, James Tell's contract was finished. He is a free man now, and I hope a wiser one."

—The End—

The Adventure of the Chess Messages

As I mentioned in some earlier stories, my wife, Mary, had insisted that I take a holiday from work. At the same time, she visited a favorite cousin in Shropshire. She had suggested that I visit my friend Sherlock Holmes and Holmes quickly agreed. Well, I have written about two cases that I worked on with Holmes while I was on that initial visit. But as it turned out. Mary's friend had a fall on the steps of her home and severely sprained her ankle. With three small children to care for, she asked Mary if she could stay another week, and my Mary agreed. My staying longer was fine with Holmes, and aside from my missing, my wife all was well.

It had been a beautiful Friday in late April, and I was returning from the tobacconist carrying the mail. As I walked into our sitting room, I had been looking at a particular letter from the Bank of England. Suddenly, Holmes's voice startled me. "You are wondering why the Bank of England sends me a letter each Friday?"

I looked down at the letters in my hand. There were five letters, and they were facing away from Holmes as

I held the top letter, the one from the Bank of England at an angle so that I might look at it.

"Confound it, Holmes," how did you know which letter of all these I was looking at.

"Well," Holmes said, taking a long pull on his black clay and sending blue fumes into the air. "I have to admit it was partially a guess. There is no way for me to tell if it were some other letter concerning me that had taken your attention enough to put a curious look on your face. I knew, however, that it was not a letter from your Mary because you always smile when you receive one from her. And your wife is, perhaps, the only one who writes to you.

"You have been here going on three weeks, and it has become your habit to fetch the mail. You look over the mail as you bring it up; I've observed you doing so, perhaps in the hope of receiving a letter from your wife.

"A letter from the Bank of England arrives each Friday, promptly. Seeing this same letter for the third time has aroused your curiosity."

"Seems simple enough now that you've explained it," I said. I enjoyed Holmes' deductions. "But what if the return address had been 'Moriarty?'"

"Touché," Holmes said with a laugh. "That would certainly, also, have explained the expression on your face, but it is nothing so interesting. Go ahead. Open the letter."

I went to the desk and from a drawer extracted a letter opener. I could feel papers inside and carefully slit the side of the envelope so as not to damage the letter's content.

Putting my fingers on the top and bottom of the envelope, I squeezed the envelope, and seven one pound bank notes slipped out into my hand. Expecting more, I shook the envelope. When nothing more emerged, I looked inside. The Seven banknotes were all that were in the envelope.

I held up the seven-pound notes and asked, "So, what is this about?"

"Payment for services, my good friend. Every week, on Friday, I receive seven pounds a collected payment from the banks of London."

"And what do you do for this payment?"

"I simply read the newspapers."

I looked at him in astonishment. "You are paid seven pounds a week to look at the papers? What that's 364 pounds a year. It's a small fortune. Why ever would they pay you this?"

"It is time-consuming work. You were not here at the time I stopped the planned robbery of the Berhieres Bank."

"I read about that in the paper. I believe Lestrade took the credit."

"Yes, he was the one who, with myself and several constables, lay in wait in the bank as the crew of criminals tunneled in. We captured them red-handed, so to speak."

"But you were the one who figured out the robber's plan?"

"It was simplicity itself. I read the papers very thoroughly. I take particular interest in messages written in code. The thieves who attempted to rob the Berhieres Bank used a simple letter substitution code in the messages they left each other in the personals section of the paper. You know if you send the paper a few pence along with a personal advertisement, they will print it. Holmes began writing on a sheet of paper.

"Many of the coded messages are married lovers setting up illicit meetings. The would-be bank robbers thought that if they communicated that way, no one would be the wiser.

"I spotted this not too long ago.

WIIFIF, LDVDWSZ LUQ H YUV XUY. BPDOH-FIOBPDH OHCJIQ

It is a series of seemingly nonsense letters spaced like actual words of varying length. As you see in this 50 character sample, there is one comma and one period. I immediately suspected it to be a 'code.'

It occurred to me that the last two letter groupings consisting of 19 characters, twelve and six with one space between them, might be a 'signature.'

"As this 'code' aroused my curiosity I kept a lookout for more messages with the same coded 'signature.'"

"It is a simple word substitution code as I found more similar messages; it became easily solvable. It translates to:" Holmes held up the sheet of paper.

"Needed, fixings for a box job. Philadelphia lawyer"

I looked down at the message. "I'm not clear on it even though it has been translated."

Holmes laughed. "Fixings are tools, a box job refers to a safe and a Philadelphia lawyer is someone considered by many to be very smart. It aroused my curiosity immediately, and I kept a lookout for more messages from BPDOHFIOBPDH OHCJIQ.

"Over a period of a fortnight, I uncovered the plan to rob the Berhieres Bank. I shared the information with Lestrade, and we caught the thieves. Although Lestrade did take credit for solving the case in the newspapers, he let the bank know of my involvement. Soon after, a representative of a number of banks approached me. They would pay me to watch out for such schemes posted under advertisements in the paper. I do so anyway, and I turned them down. So they had Mycroft approach me."

"And he convinced you?"

"No, a personal request from her majesty convinced me."

And that was it for the conversation at the time. Holmes does not believe in coincidence, but it was serendipity that the Tuesday after I returned from a trip to my tobacconist and was stopped by Mrs. Hudson in the entryway.

"Doctor," Mrs. Hudson whispered, "A very agitated young man, a massive young man, just ran up the steps to your rooms. I don't know what he wants, but he seemed very upset. Do you think I should call the police?"

It took me only a moment to assess the situation. Wait here. If I do not come to the top of the stairs within a minute's time, do go and summon the police.

With that plan in place, I climbed the stairs quickly and burst into Holmes' apartment. Had I my Webley with me, I would have drawn it, but it was at the time in my room. As I entered, ready for anything, I found a very tall young man, topping six feet, six inches, with a mop of blonde hair, bulging blue eyes, and an almost wild way about him, pacing Holmes' sitting room in a circle. Holmes sat unmoved in his lounge chair and was calmly lighting his pipe.

"Watson," Holmes cried, "May I introduce Hieronymus Grayling. Mr. Grayling is the potentate of the London Chess Enthusiasts Club, and he has come to us with a problem regarding chess."

"Chess?" I said, physically relaxing, now that I knew I would not have to go into battle with this giant.

"Well, that's just it," Grayling said. His voice was high-pitched for such a large man, and it seemed a bit disconcerting. "What is listed as chess in the paper is apparently not, or not any type of chess that I have ever seen." With that, he drew a folded newspaper from his Norfolk jacket. He handed the newspaper over to Holmes and pointed to an item on the open page. I saw as I moved behind Holmes' chair, that the item was a long advertisement in the personals section of the paper. It appeared to be a chess game. The announcement read:

RESULTS OF THE IRISH CHESS TOURNAMENT

between Roy O'Hearn and Boyd Flynn

The game will continue Saturday.

c2-c3 c7-c6

c3xc7 e7-e6

f2-f5 a7-a5

Q-d6

Kb8-c4

a2-a5 B-b3

e2-e5 a1xa5

b2-b3

B-a3

N-c5Bxb3

B-b4

A5-a4

Q-a5 B-a3

h2-h6 f7-f4

d4-d4 Qxf4

h2-h4 b2-b5

Kb1-a3 K-c4

K-c5 c7-c5

K-g4 B-b4

B2-b5 R-h6

K-g5

e7-e6

Q-h5g7-g6
d7-d6 d2-d6

"This makes no sense at all, Mr. Holmes," Grayling said.

Holmes scanned the listing. I suddenly remembered Mrs. Hudson. I rushed out of the room and caught her going down the street to fetch a constable. When I got back, Holmes was reassuring Mr. Grayling.

"This does not appear to be a chess match at all, Mr. Grayling. It appears to be something entirely different, and I will look into it. And I do appreciate your bringing it to my attention."

When our visitor had left, Holmes did not keep me waiting. "This appears to be a secret code of some sort. And as I am hired to break such codes, I must get to work on it. I won't know if this involves one of my banks until I check.

I left Holmes puzzling over the chess match listing when I retired. In the morning, I found him gazing out the window in thought.

"Did you solve the puzzle?" I asked.

"Yes, I did. And it appears to be about an attempt to rob an unspecified London bank."

"Does it say when?" I asked.

"The note is actually about a meeting where the participants will discuss the robbery." He tossed me a sheet of notepaper. "The message is decoded there."

Meet For London Bank

Job 9:15 p

Black Pig Thurs

"The Black Pig is a pub I take it?" I asked.

"Yes. And if I'm not mistaken, it has not been open for a few years."

"How did the code work?"

"Whoever devised this code made it reasonably simple. They assumed, quite correctly, except for the intercession of Mr. Grayling, that no-one would be interested in a private chess match, much less those of some Irishmen. It was merely a matter of figuring out how the keyboard worked.

"A chessboard is divided into an 8 x 8 grid. Two rows on the bottom and two on the top denote the playing pieces. I simply had to decode what letters the rest of the boxes stood for. This is what I came up with. I did not include the 4 rows of pieces in row 7 and 8 and 2 and 1." He put another scrap of paper in from of me. It was quickly clear the number at the beginning of each row of letters indicated a chessboard row number.

6 q w e r t y u I
5 o p a s d f g h
4 j k l : z X c v
3 b n m

"I simply used the common typewriting machine keyboard as a starting point. The chess game was obviously a deception, as moves were made that would have been impossible in a real game. There are no numbers, so the would-be thieves used Roman Numerals. The time 9:15p was written as ix:vp. The colon was the only punctuation mark I was able to decode as no other punctuation was used. The key or letter was whatever square the piece landed on. The odd breakup of the moves was a simple way to denote a space between words."

"I assume you will inform Scotland Yard?"

Holmes looked at me and smiled. "In good time, Watson, in good time."

I looked at Holmes for a long moment. I had known him long enough to make a good guess at what he was planning."

"You are planning to go to the meeting. In one of your disguises, I'd imagine."

"Watson, you never cease to amaze me with your own deductive ability," Holmes said.

I felt myself reddening, embarrassed though pleased at the compliment.

"So, my assumption is correct."

"No, Watson. It was close, but not correct. You, Watson, will go to the meeting place and try to get close enough to the thieves to overhear their plan. I unfortunately have something else I must do at 9:15 Thursday night.

Holmes quickly got to work with his collection of newspapers. In addition to British papers, he subscribed to ones from Scotland, Wales, and Ireland. By mid-afternoon, he had determined that Alastair McGruell, if it is his real name, for I have no knowledge of a criminal by that name, would be coming to the meeting via secret chess messages in the Glasgow Herald newspaper.

"But won't they know this, McGruell?" I asked.

"No," Holmes replied. "That was the beauty of the plan of the mastermind of this operation. It is likely none of the participants in the crime know each other. They were recruited via the paper—I have no doubt they were at some point propositioned by mail with their reply submitted by newspaper personals. If they replied in the positive, they were sent the code, which was then used to update plans via the newspapers."

I thought a moment. "Wouldn't it have been easier to just correspond via the mail?"

"Yes, but this method was, I believed, deemed safer, and had the advantage of allowing for last-minute changes. Unfortunately for them, and fortunately for us, Grayling came to us about the chess moves in the paper. Unfortunately for us, I do not know Alastair McGruell by sight."

Knowing that McGruell had been instructed to spend as little time in London as possible, Holmes concluded, after studying the train schedules, that McGruell would be arriving by train from Glasgow on Thursday afternoon around 2:15. Holmes, Lestrade, and I were in wait for him at the station. Lestrade had a paddy wagon parked nearby.

The man Holmes identified as McGruell when he emerged from the train looked enough like me to cause me some surprise. In build, carriage, and hairstyle, and even dress, we could have been brothers. As instructed, I approached the stranger. He had been looking back at the train car as I tapped him on the shoulder. He turned in surprise and glared at me.

"What do you want?" he demanded loudly.

"Mr. McGruell," I whispered. "There has been a change in the plan. If you are still interested, you should follow me." With that, I turned and walked away and headed toward the terminal. I did not look back or try to persuade him to follow. As Holmes predicted, the man was soon on my heel."

"What is going on," he demanded though not as loudly as he had required my business."

"Not here," I whispered back harshly. "There is a private place up ahead where we can talk."

I had no sooner entered the seemingly deserted and dark supply room when there was a loud slapping sound like leather hitting flesh, and McGruell, who had been practically walking in my footsteps, fell against me.

As Holmes struggled to hold up the unconscious man, Lestrade protested loudly, "There was no need for that! I would have had him under control."

"Help me! Grab him, Lestrade! Watson," Holmes shouted. "Whatever you do, don't let him hit the ground." And in an instant, both he, Lestrade, and I grabbed the body of the slumping McGruell and eased him to the ground. It was then I saw the leather billy in Holmes's hand.

"Let me check him," I said, but Holmes blocked me from the man with an arm.

"Not just yet, Watson. I noticed his coat and his right hand as he came in. This coat has burns and discolored threads from nitric and sulfuric acid. And his hand was holding his front pocket."

Lestrade carefully began searching the man's pockets, starting with his coat.

"Very carefully," Holmes warned Lestrade.

Lestrade looked at Holmes but then patted the man's body more softly.

"Found something," Lestrade said, "feels like a bottle."

"Easy, Lestrade! Take it out very easily," Holmes said urgently.

While I looked on, completely puzzled, shocked that Holmes without provocation had rendered the man unconscious, Lestrade eased a small bottle from the man's front pocket.

"Turn on a lamp if you please, Watson," Holmes commanded.

I did as he said and turned back to my companions.

Lestrade held the bottle up for Holmes and I to inspect. A handwritten label on the bottle said Nitro. Holmes took it carefully from Lestrade.

"That's not?" I said.

"Yes, Watson. Nitroglycerin!" He looked down at the face of the man on the floor who had a large muff of graying whiskers about the face. "McGruell my foot, the beard is new, but this is McAlester, Peter McAlester, the nitro man. He is known for always carrying a small bottle with him. Lestrade, you'd better make sure he does not have another.

Lestrade continued his search of the unconscious man.

"Did you suspect that this McAlester was the one coming?"

Holmes nodded. "I thought there was a good chance of it being him. They would need a nitro man to get into a vault, and McAlester is known as one of the best."

"And you did not tell me? I could have been killed."

"Your situation would have been more dangerous if you'd given any sign of fear. And you were our only choice. Lestrade looks like a policeman, and I was known to the man."

Lestrade stood; satisfied he had searched the man thoroughly. "That's the only bottle. I'm surprised he didn't have a revolver."

"He didn't need one with that bottle as a weapon."

"What are we going to do with it, Holmes? I, for one, don't want to be carrying it about."

"Very simple, actually," Holmes said. He carefully opened the bottle, and lowering it to floor level poured it out. The liquid spread and formed a puddle on the floor. Extracting one of the new red phosphorus matches, he lit the match and touched it to the pool of liquid. It ignited like a puddle of coal oil. It burned quickly and then went out.

"We can refill the bottle with olive oil when we get a chance Watson, that should have the correct color. But first, let's make sure it is empty."

Flicking the open bottle, mouth first toward the floor, two drops flew out. As they hit the floor, each created a bright flash and loud bang. Both Lestrade and I jumped back.

"You can imagine what the entire bottle would do."

Holmes handed me the bottle. I looked it over carefully to be sure it was completely empty before reaching down to slip it into my pocket. Holmes stuck out a hand to block me.

"Not your pocket, old boy. You need to change clothes with McGruell first."

At 9:11, that little bottle was secure in the pocket of McAlester's coat safely filled with oil provided by Mrs. Hudson. I was worried about my own good clothing on a strange criminal somewhere hidden within the bowels of Scotland Yard. That I needed McAlester's coat, I now understood, for the pockets contained fuses and various incendiary devices that were probably needed in his profession.

Holmes had spent the morning with some of the street ruffians he called his irregulars, and the afternoon playing his violin. At 8:00 p.m., he and I had taken a hansom to within two blocks of the train station. There, we separated, and I had walked to the train station and found another hansom to take me as close to the Black Pig as the cab driver dared. The Pig was at the end of a little dead-end alley, and the driver refused to venture into it. There were no street lamps. Only moonlight lit the cul-de-sac. I approached what had once been the drinking establishment on foot. Its doors and windows were boarded over. Not a soul was in the alley but for a drunken old man sleeping against a wall in the entryway. Not knowing what else to do, I went to the grimy door and knocked softly. An instant later, an arm grabbed me about the chest, and a knife was pressed against my throat.

"What a we got here?" a squeaky voice intoned. "A citizen nosing around where he don't belong?"

For a moment, panic held me. Was I being mugged? But then reason came back to me. I reached into my coat pocket.

"I have something of value you can take if you let me go," I said.

"Let's have it then," he demanded, but neither moved his knife or his arm.

I extracted my bottle and held it down behind me. "This is nitro, you fool. Harm me, and I drop it. The birds'll be picking pieces of us off the street for days."

"Easy! Easy now," the man said, letting me go. "Was just testing to see if you belonged. We've been waiting on you. You are the last to arrive. This way," he said, pointing.

We went through a tiny passageway alongside the Black Pig and emerged on another street. A dark growler was waiting there. My new companion swung into the door of that carriage with a wave to the tall thin driver who was dressed entirely in black with a black kerchief in front of his face. The driver seemed to eye me with suspicion as I climbed into the carriage. His glare, if he was indeed a he, made me uncomfortable. I had been involved with Holmes for some time and had met many criminals. I could only hope the driver was not one of the ones I had met.

Inside the carriage, the shades were drawn. In the dim light, I sensed the shapes of two additional men. I was glad the shades were drawn. I might have met either of the two in the course of Holmes' cases.

We had gone a short distance in the carriage when the man who had brought me to it lit a match and then held it to a cigarette. I turned my face toward the shaded window. In the match-light, I caught a glimpse of a face across from me. He was familiar to me, but I could not remember from where. He was an older man, and his skin was drawn. He had the pallor of a convict newly released from the stir. I feared he was someone I had helped Holmes put in prison.

It was only moments later that the cab pulled to a stop. My companion gestured for me to exit the carriage first. I opened the door and stepped out.

We were in front of an establishment called Poor Child's Boot Maker. The street lamps were bright enough to make the sign clearly visible. There was a chill in the air, and I lifted my scarf up and covered the lower portion of my face. The other three from the carriage joined me. The driver stayed where he was in the carriage.

"Come on," the man who had brought me to the carriage, apparently the leader, said. He walked up to the boot maker's and opened the door with a key. A sign in the window said: "Off on Holiday back May 1st."

Boots and shoes hung or sat on every surface. There was a smell of leather in the air. Once inside, our leader lit a lamp and entered a doorway to the back of the snob's shop. There he led us to another door, which was open to a stairway going down. We had entered in single file, and so far, the man I thought I recognized had not seen my face. I kept my head down and quickly descended the narrow stairway after the leader.

At the bottom of the stairway, a room opened. As far as I could tell, the floor was dirt. Still, there were wooden cases covering most of it, piled with leather scraps, worn laces, the debris of a snob who apparently never threw anything away. I was confused as to why we were there until the leader walked to a corner and turned. The basement was l-shaped, and at the end of the L, there was a hole carved into the wall. Beyond it was a tunnel. This is where the man led me. The tunnel was only about 20 feet long and maybe four feet high. I had to crouch down to follow him. It smelled of earth, and when I stood too high, my hat brushed the tunnel's ceiling, and dirt fell. I had a sudden image of the entire tunnel collapsing. As if reading my mind, the man turned. "Don't worry, it'll hold long enough," he said.

The tunnel opened again into a room. Three oil lamps lighted it inside. It took me only a moment to surmise we were in a bank. On my right, a massive steel door was set into the wall.

"I've already done the drilling for ya," my companion said. Although all of the men in the carriage but for the driver had come into the boot maker's, none had ventured into the tunnel, I could see their silhouettes at the far end. I looked at the vault door. Five holes had been drilled around the lock mechanism.

"Looks like a good job," I said. He seemed please with my praise. "Best you go back down the tunnel."

"I can stay and help," the man said. "I'd like to learn, and you are the best."

"I am flattered, but if I teach you, it won't be while on the job. I work alone."

The man nodded. As he began to walk away, I looked around the room. There was a door at the far end of the wall. I assumed it lead to a stairway up to the bank. "Wait," I said. "Is that door locked?" I gestured toward the door.

"Don't know," he said, "But there is a good chance they have one of those new-fangled alarms on it, so we left it alone."

I nodded. He nodded back, and I watched him go back down the tunnel. I looked at that door for a long moment.

McAlester, in addition to the nitro, had the tools of his trade in the pockets of his long coat. In addition to long bits of fuse and firecracker-like caps, there was a little funnel with a small tube connected. Holmes, Lestrade, and I had spent some time going over the items.

The men at the end of the tunnel were watching. I removed the funnel from one pocket and the bottle of nitro from another. I opened the bottle and very slowly placed it on top of the lock itself. The holes the leader had drilled had been placed around the locking mechanism in a clock-like circle. I made a show of inserting the tube into the hole at 12 o'clock, then taking the bottle and carefully pouring in enough of my fake nitro to fill the hole almost to the top. Holmes had prepped me, though how he had come by the knowledge, I do not know. Care had to be taken to remove the tube without any droplets falling. I did this by holding a finger over the end of the tube and then carefully moving the end of the tube to the next hole.

I thought of my situation. Holmes, Lestrade, and I had thought that this was to be a planning meeting. Once we knew the plan, police would be ready to move in when the bank robbers struck. Instead, the meeting had turned out to be the actual bank robbery. There were no police waiting to move in. And my situation was precarious at best. Holmes had insisted I not bring my Webley's revolver, arguing that McAlester never carried one. But now I was defenseless. A man who would recognize me was at the end of the tunnel and would see me when I emerged from it. At best, they would simply detain me. But when my "nitro" failed to explode, my fate might be sealed.

After finishing filling the last hole, I carefully lifted the funnel and tube, put my finger over the end of the tube, and made a show of placing the tube end in the bottle and emptying any last drops back into the bottle. Then I screwed the cap back on the bottle and slipped it into my pocket. I had two choices. I could go back down the tunnel and try to make it to the stairs before they thought to stop me. Or I could try my luck with the door to the upper levels of the bank. There were two problems with the bank door. One, it might be locked, and my immediate associates might wonder about my trying a door that might set off an alarm. On the other hand, an alarm might save my life, as no one knew where I was.

I tried to make a decision as I put a cap in each of the holes and connected a short fuse to each. These short pieces were flash fuses, Holmes had explained. When the main burning fuse reached them, they would all burn very rapidly to set off all the charges at once. Using some sticky tape, I connected the main fuse to the five flash fuses. They formed a circle around the main fuse. The main fuse that McAlester carried was about six feet long. Holmes had explained that it would give me slightly more than one minute once the far end was lit before the flash fuses caught and set off the caps.

I held the end of the fuse in my hand. My heart beat rapidly as I stuck a match and ignited the end of the long wick. As the fuse sputtered, smoked, and flared, I dropped the end and began running.

I had thought that I would run toward the bank robbers and yell for them to get up the stairs and hope that the man who I thought I recognized would not recognize me in that situation. But instead, almost to my own surprise, I found myself running toward the door to the bank. My heart was beating wildly. If the door was locked, my fate might well be sealed. The men at the far end of the tunnel were watching. If they saw me trying to escape, they would most likely kill me.

I grabbed the door handle and turned it. To my joy and surprise, it turned, and the door swung easily open.

Then my luck turned. A loud, blaring alarm began sounding. It sounded almost like a foghorn. I knew some banks had alarms powered by containers of compressed air but had never heard one before. But this was just the first of the bad luck. Beyond the door that had easily opened was a heavy metal gate. And a colossal padlock locked this gate. I shook the gate hard, just in case, for some reason, that might help. But shaking the gate only served to reinforce the fact that I could not go this way.

Feeling panicked, I ran in the direction of the waiting men. As I approached them, I yelled, "Run! Run! It is going to blow any second."

All but the leader turned and headed for the stairway. The leader stood there waiting for me, an angry gleam in his eye and, I saw as I came closer to him, he held a revolver in his right hand."

"What are you doing at that door?" He demanded. "I told you it were alarmed?

"Blast force! Run, you fool?"

96

He had put out a hand to stop me, but my cry half turned him as I rushed by. I turned my head and ran toward the stairway. He began to follow.

"I had to put more nitro than is safe in the door. It's too thick for any less. But it will be one heck of a bang. And with that door closed, this was the only way the blast force could go! Did you want to collapse the tunnel?"

"But the alarm>?" He protested.

"How long will it take you to grab the loot once the door is open. I figure we have ten minutes."

"You better be right," he warned as we both hurriedly climbed the stairway.

I braced myself to be facing the man whom I had seen before and was wondering how successful I'd be in making a run for it when we cleared the top of the stairs. I ran for the open door of the snob's and bolted through. There I stopped in my tracks. Holmes and Lestrade were there along with a few uniformed police. The gang members, including the driver, were all kneeling on the floor with their hands on their heads. One, a middle-aged man with short grey hair, stared at me. He was the one I recognized. The man gave me a dirty look and spit on the floor. He knew me too. Lestrade and Holmes brought their revolvers up, pointed past me. From behind me, there came a snarl as the leader learned he was trapped. I felt a push that toppled me to my side and sent me to the floor. A moment later, there was a crash as a young policeman tackled the leader and brought him down.

"Watch," Holmes warned. "That's Gunner Shomes, he'll have a revolver on him."

The young policeman, pulled Gunner's arms behind him, applied handcuffs, and then quickly searched him for weapons. Gunner twisted and turned, and soon the revolver he had recently pointed at me clattered to the floor. Lestrade picked it up.

A series of popping sounds so close they were like one long gunshot came from the basement. I knew the fuses had burned to the caps.

"Once we realized this was the bank robbery itself, not just a meeting about it, I locked the bank gate," Holmes explained once we were back in Baker Street.

I looked at him in surprise.

"We needed the men to go out by the bootmaker's. We had officers with us, but only so many. Lestrade did not want them going out in different directions."

He paused and smiled at me. "There was a one-armed officer there, but he was hidden. I did not think to show him a picture of you, just in case you tried alone to exit that way. An unfortunate oversight on my part."

"But how did you know where I was? Or what bank they were robbing? I saw no one following me," I asked.

"You saw me meeting with my irregulars that morning. I set them out for two purposes; one was to roam around the local banks looking for signs of dirt, which had been dumped. I assumed that the robbers would have to use a tunnel to enter whatever bank they were going to try and rob. And that the tunnel digging was already in progress. The outside doors of the banks are watched by patrolmen on duty and have alarms. A tunnel made the best sense. But a tunnel means dirt that must be disposed of. My irregulars found the soil and thus the bank.

"It had always seemed odd to me that a meeting at this point was necessary. So I was prepared in case the actual bank robbery proceeded this evening. Lestrade was ready with his men.

"But we did not know where the criminals had dug their tunnel. So my irregulars were also tasked with keeping an eye on you. I had boys stationed all around the Black Pig. Children seem to be so innocuous that few even notice them.

"They observed you getting into the carriage and even exiting at the bootmaker's. We knew where you were minutes after your arrival there," Holmes said proudly. "As we already knew which bank they were going to rob, Lestrade, his men, and I were already in the immediate area."

"How many of your irregulars did you employ?" I asked.

"Thirty," Homes said. "And worth every penny I paid them," he paused a moment and then continued. "We simply needed you to lead us to the tunnel."

"You know I was in considerable danger," I said. "One of the men recognized me."

"That would be Jack Spikkel. We arrested him together some years ago, and he apparently had not forgotten either of us. I am sorry for that, Watson. But I had no way of knowing the composition of the bank crew."

He was silent for the moment, and I was contemplating the close call I had had.

"Overall," Holmes said. "This case did have some interesting features. What do you think you'll call it in your memoirs, Watson?

—The End—

The Adventure of the Numerologist's Cypher

As I mentioned in some earlier stories, my wife, Mary, had insisted that I take a holiday from work. At the same time, she visited a favorite cousin in Shropshire. She had suggested that I visit my friend Sherlock Holmes and Holmes quickly agreed. Well, I have written about some cases that I worked on with Holmes while I was on that initial visit. But as it turned out. Mary's friend had a fall on the steps of her home and severely sprained her ankle. With three small children to care for, she asked Mary if she could stay another week, and my Mary agreed. Mary's friend, however, did not recover, and Mary sent a telegram begging that I come and look into the situation. As it turned out, the local physician was a drinking man and had misdiagnosed Mary's friend's condition. The ankle was broken. I reset it and agreed Mary should stay on for as long as it took for the friend to recover. The visit was pleasant in that I had missed my wife and so my visit was thus enjoyable.

Holmes told me I was welcome for as long as I liked. I was thinking about reopening my practice when a case came along for which Holmes required my assistance.

It was on an early morning in May of 1890, the day after my return when Mrs. Hudson ushered a young man into Holmes' apartment. He was better dressed than most of our visitors, wore glasses with gold wire-frames, on a fish-like face, and had a stock of well-groomed dark hair. His expression was most serious. In his thin hands, he held a worn looking leather case, which was, tied shut.

"What brings a successful barrister to our humble home?" Holmes asked.

The young man was taken aback. "Why would you assume I'm a successful barrister?" the man asked.

Holmes smiled. "I recognize the case. Your uncle's, I presume?"

"Yes, it was," the man said.

"I know him, read recently of his retirement, and am sure he would not pass it off to just anyone. As to your success, your clothing speaks to that. If you were a mere assistant, you would most likely dress well given your social status but probably not so well."

"Simple," the man scoffed.

I found myself feeling irritated at the young man. I have often thought that Holmes's deductions do seem simple once explained. Still, the young man's dismissal of them seemed condescending.

"My time is valuable, too, Mr. Wycoss. Please tell us why you are here?"

The man was taken aback again. I assumed because Holmes knew his name. But even I knew of the retired barrister, a life-long bachelor, and also knew his sister was married to a man named Wycoss. The entire story had been in a recent edition of the Times.

"I represent the new Earl of Bashlessing. His uncle, having recently died, left him, along with the estate, a paper purported to be the key to a treasure the late

Earl brought back from the Congo many years ago." From the letter case, the young man produced a piece of paper so worn it resembled parchment. Across it were printed a series of numbers.

"Apparently, the Earl was a numerologist. He left the instructions for recovering the items he brought back from the Congo in a numerological code. I think he assumed that young Peter would remember how to decipher it. Peter had been put in the Earl's care when he was nine after his parents were both killed in a boating incident. Apparently, the Earl doted on the boy. But the Earl and his wife separated when the boy was 11, and the Duchess took Peter and his younger sister with her to Italy. The Duchess died a year ago. There were plans for Peter, his sister, Ann, and the Earl to reunite this summer, but the Earl died before the reunion could take place. Unfortunately, Peter does not remember anything about any code the uncle may have shared with him as a boy. He was at his wit's end until someone suggested you might be able to solve it."

Holmes studied the piece of paper carefully. I glanced over. There were twelve lines of numbers. Each number was made up of six numerals. The numbers on the lines varied from two on the shortest line to seven on the longest.

049066 101005 099205 102130
112201 101050
045097 103201 101059 102139 057049 203101
071062
102013 087226 249262
402010 099106 188152 101041 122020
058354 111094 099241 068074 014128
099313 199006 251089 001141 111031
075076 223090 299122 047293
177226 123019 233197 069073 006298

247156 188026 192319
123028 076138 186154 140002
121030 212101 099322 213127

"Can you decipher it?" Wycoss asked. There was a touch of impertinence to his question that I had to keep myself from responding to.

"I believe I can, but I would like a day or two to consider it."

Wycoss begrudgingly nodded.

I started to stand up, but Holmes stopped me by putting a hand on my arm.

"Well, I will leave you to it," Wycoss said as he turned to leave.

"I take it you have spoken to young Peter?" Holmes asked.

The man turned again with an annoyed look. "Of course!"

"Would you kindly ask him if he remembers his Uncle's favorite number?" Holmes asked. "And let me know his answer as soon as possible?"

"I will do that, and telegraph you his reply," Wycoss said before exiting.

"I say, Holmes. What a rude fellow."

"He's young, Watson. The young are duty-bound to make mistakes."

"What do you make of the puzzle?" I asked, pointing to the paper.

Holmes glanced at the paper. "Child's play. There may be more to this than what appears. There may even be sinister aspects. I am anxiously awaiting Wycoss's reply to my query about the Earl's favorite number."

The telegram came early the next morning. I was enjoying a late sleep-in when Holmes roused me. "Watson, get dressed. We must hurry. The real Peter Bash-lessing may still be alive."

He held the telegram out in his hand. I read it quick-ly.

Peter can't seem to remember his uncle's favorite number, sorry.

It was signed by Julian Wycoss.

"But how can you know Peter Bashlessing may be in danger from this telegram?" I asked, quite confounded.

"Watson, it's the code. Didn't you notice that in every one of those six-digit numbers, if you add the digits to-gether, they add up to seven? Seven was obviously the Earl's favorite number. I hoped that if the real Earl was still alive and had heard of me, he'd send me a clue. He did by saying he couldn't remember his uncle's fa-vorite number.

Holmes explained how he deciphered the code on the train ride to Bashlessing.

"Numerologists add numbers together to find the base number. If you take a number like 049066, the digits add up to seven. That is four plus nine equals 13. One plus three equals 4. The six, if added to the six becomes twelve, which when the one and two is added becomes 3. Add the 3 to the four, and you get 7.

Now, obviously, we need a way to have 26 letters. For every six-letter number in the code, if you add the first three numbers to the last three, you get a three-digit number. The Earl used these to get an alphabet. He laid a sheet of notepaper out before me, which deci-phered the code.

106 A ^101005 ^057049
115 B ^102013 ^049066
124 C
133 D ^071062

142 E ^101041 ^122020 ^068074 ^045097 ^014128
^001141 ^111031 ^123019 ^069073 ^140002
151 F ^101050 ^075076 ^123028 ^121030
160 G ^101059
205 H ^099106 ^111094 ^199006
214 I ^188026 ^076138
223 J
232 K ^102130
241 L ^102139
250 M
304 N ^099205 ^103201 ^203101 ^006298
313 O ^112201 ^087226 ^223090 ^212101
322 P
331 Q
340 R ^188152 ^099241 ^251089 ^047293 ^213127
403 S ^177226 ^247156
412 T ^402010 ^058354 ^099313
421 U ^299122 ^099322
430 V ^233197 ^122308 ^186154
502 W
511 X ^249262 ^192319
520 Y
601 Z

The message read:

Bank of England box

THREE THREE THREE FOUR SEVEN SIX FIVE FOUR

The Earl's treasure is in a private box at the bank, but I think our duty is to save the Earl's real treasure, a favorite nephew.

Holmes had sent a return telegram to Wycoss, letting him know he should inform his client that Holmes and I would be visiting Bashlessing to speak to the young Earl himself. He had concluded the telegram by saying: With just a few more questions, I am sure we can unravel the key to the hidden treasure.

"We need to leave, Watson. Do bring your revolver."

We took the 4:02 train and arrived in Bashlessing at 6:04. A young man of about 15 years approached us and offered to help us with our luggage.

"We have no luggage," Holmes said, "but perhaps you can aid us in another way. We need a reliable lad to run an errand later."

"I am your man, sir," the boy said.

"What is your name?" Holmes asked.

"Connor, sir."

"Well, Connor, can you first tell me if there is a doctor in the village?"

"No, sir. I mean, yes, sir, but he ain't here."

A quizzical look on Holmes' part brought an explanation.

"Mrs. Farington is having a baby, sir. The doc went out there just an hour ago. She's got six, and it takes her a bit a time to push'em out."

Pleased Holmes gave the boy his instructions, a half-crown, and was directed to where we could rent a cart.

Less than a half-hour later, riding through thick forest the entire way, we arrived at Bashlessing Manor, which appeared around the bend of the road. The home was large, sprawling, built of stone and oak as befitted an Earl. Our knock at the door was met by a large, imposing man with a balding head. Sherlock gave his business, and we were ushered inside and seated on opulent chairs before a large fireplace in which a small fire was burning. Before long, a tall, slim young man with reddish hair appeared.

Holmes and I rose. "Lord Bashlessing," Holmes said with a slight bow.

106

"Peter will do," the young man said. "I've never gone into the peerage protocols."

"Refreshing," Holmes said.

I shook the young man's hand. His grip was firm enough, but his hand was perspiring.

"Let's get down to business shall we," Holmes continued.

"By all means," The young Earl waved us to seats pulled a chair up, so we were just a few feet apart.

"I have brought Dr. Watson because he had been dabbling in Hypnosis of late.

It was news to me, and I had to concentrate to not look surprised.

"Tomorrow, as it is best to do it in the morning, he will hypnotize you, and I think with luck that way, we may be able to get the code solved. I have an urgent appointment back in London this evening, but I will leave him here to work his magic. But there is even better news. I was able to locate your childhood Nanny, Patricia Freeman. She will be arriving the day after tomorrow. And if Dr. Watson's hypnosis does not work, she may remember how the cypher works. If, for example, it is a book code based on a favorite book, where the numbers refer to the locations of words on a specific page, she may remember the book. We could not go into it in detail in telegrams but did say your favorite number was 4."

I was watching the young man's face as Holmes told him this. If the mention of hypnosis caused a brief flicker of concern, the mention of the nanny arriving in two days, caused a much longer one.

It was then that the servant returned. "There is a village boy a the door saying that he has an urgent message for Dr. Watson.

"Who would know you are here?" the Earl asked, suspiciously.

"A young man named Connor helped find a cart and gave directions at the station," I said.

"It is Connor, sir," the servant said.

"Show him in, then."

Young Connor was ushered in, out of breath, and with a dire expression on his face. "Dr. Watson, can you come back to the village. Ned Deems fell and broke his leg badly. His bones sticking out through the skin."

"Can't Dr. Anderson tend the man?" the Earl asked.

"He's out at Mrs. Farington's helping her with the new'n."

"Actually, our business is done, for now, your Lordship," Holmes said. "Doctor Watson can see to the man, stay in the village if necessary and be back out in the morning for the hypnosis. I, as I mentioned, have to return to London."

Not long after, Holmes, Connor, and myself were riding the cart away from the estate. Holmes was driving. When we were out of sight after the second turn of the road, Holmes stopped the carriage. After instructing Connor to take the cart all the way to town, we made our way through the woods until we had a view of both the front entrance and the servants' entrance.

"That young man is not a member of the aristocracy. He doesn't have the breeding or the manners," Holmes said. "He has the hands of someone who has spent many of his early years on a farm.

"Then, where is the real Earl?"

"I am hoping hidden away as a prisoner. The realm is very unforgiving of those who would murder a member of the peerage. In fact, it is one of Mycroft's duties to handle that should it occur. On the other hand, a mere thief can sometimes be gotten away with. But more than that, I don't think our imposter would dispatch the young Earl if his help might be needed to solve the cypher."

"But the real Earl hasn't given up the code yet?" I asked.

"No. And the imposter chose to try and have the code decoded rather than resort to extreme means, until now. But with the threat of the Nanny coming, the imposter will have to force the real Earl to reveal the secret of the code."

We were rewarded two hours later when a tall, slim figure dressed in black exited the front entrance of the estate in the moonlight.

"Quickly, Watson. We must not lose sight of him."

The woods gave us adequate cover as we followed the man down a twisting lane. It was our luck that the moon was nearly full. About a mile from the manor, the man left the lane and entered a narrow track that led off into the trees.

"Have your revolver ready, Watson," Holmes said. And began hurrying toward the track. Though narrow, the track was well worn, and within a short time, we heard a door open and close. A moment later, a small cottage appeared before us.

"This must be the game keeper's. We have no time to lose."

With that, Holmes rushed to the door. A swift kick sent the door crashing inwards. In the room, a large, burly man stood behind a tall thin man who was tied to a chair. The man who had identified himself to us as the Earl held a red-hot fire poker in his hand and was approaching the man in the chair.

"Stop, whoever you are," Holmes demanded.

All three men turned toward us. The imposter, on seeing he had been caught rushed toward his prisoner with the poker. I fired a shot without even thinking about it. The poker flew from his hands as my shot took the man in the shoulder.

The large burly man backed away from the Earl of Bashlessing with his hands raised.

"Please tend to our prisoners, while I free the Earl," Holmes said.

A week later, Mrs. Hudson came to the door with two packages. One was addressed to Holmes and one to me. We opened our respective parcels to find we had each received one large diamond. The story was that Peter Bashlessing had met the young man, David Pierce, in Italy. They resembled one another, became fast friends, and the Earl unwittingly shared family stories. These stories led David to believe he could impersonate the Earl when news that Peter's uncle had died arrived. It was probably the story of the treasure in diamonds, which had tempted the young man to impersonate the Earl. It was rumored that Peter Bashlessing, Earl of Bashlessing, had recovered over 200 such gems from a box in the Bank of England. Holmes and I were scheduled for an audience with her majesty to receive a commendation. We had expected nothing from the Earl himself. Enclosed with our diamonds was a short note.

101050 112201 188152
177226 057049 233197 188026 099205 101059
000250 101041
000322 122020 402010 068074 099241
—The End—

The Adventure of Colonel Mustard's Secret

After dealing with the spy Von Bork in London in my story entitled "His Last Bow," Holmes persuaded me to visit his cottage in South Downs before heading home. This is what I did, and the one day visit was an enjoyable one even if I did have to feign a more enthusiastic interest in beekeeping than I actually entertained.

Somehow, perhaps it was fate, though, in fact, it may have been my comment that I'd like to see the sea, we ended heading out for Holmes' favorite southern beach in England. We found lodgings at a pub near Blackpool Sands that gave us easy access to the beach and had been strolling along it when a child's voice rang out behind us, shouting, "Mr. Holmes! Mr. Holmes? Is that indeed you mister Sherlock Holmes?"

We stopped, and a thin young lad in green shorts and a short-sleeve shirt, with sun-lightened brownish hair, and spectacles came to a stop next to us. His left ear was swollen as if he'd been recently struck there. He puffed for a moment out of breath by his exertions to catch up and asked, quite gentlemanly like, "Do I have the pleasure of addressing Mr. Sherlock Holmes?"

"You do," Holmes said. "And what brings a young man from Balsall Heath other than the boxed ear obviously inflicted by a stranger to seek Sherlock Holmes?"

The boy's eyes widened. "How'd you know I'm from Balsall, sir? I mean, I've read everything Dr. Watson has written bout you," he said, nodding to me. "But how'd you know that."

"I made a study of button makers. Your shirt, hand made, has Balsall buttons. They usually only sell locally. As to the boxed ear being inflicted by a stranger, you have no other visible bruises on your arms, legs, or head. So it isn't likely you are often beaten at home. Therefore the person who boxed your ear was a stranger."

"Not totally, sir. He was a policeman."

"Why did a policeman box your ear?" I asked. "And while I'm here, let me look at it." The boy turned to me. The swelling was going down. Without light, I could not look inside the ear channel, but there was no sign of bleeding, and that was a good sign.

"I saw a woman on the beach running. There were two men after her. One, the older of the two, I assume as he had grey hair, fired a pistol at her, and she fell. The other man, the bigger and I assume younger of the two, with dark hair, ran toward the fallen woman seeming very upset. Fearing they'd see me, I ran as fast as I could to the police. Officer Marlowe came back to investigate. But when we got the beach the woman was gone. When Officer Marlowe couldn't find any sign of blood, he cuffed me, said I'd made up the story."

"But you did not make it up, did you?" Holmes asked.

"No, sir."

Holmes nodded to the boy and looked at me, his eyebrow raised.

"Show us to where you saw this woman," I said. "And, as you seemed to know who we are, perhaps you should introduce yourself.

"Tony Pratt, sir. I just turned 11 on August 10th."

"On holiday with your family?" Holmes asked.

"Yes, sir. My mother thought we might not get another for a long time with the war."

Blackpool Sands is a crescent moon of a beach between green cliffs that rise above crashing waves. Young Pratt led Holmes and I to the far eastern end of the beach. We threaded our way through rocks, to where the last cliff jutted out, protecting the beach from the sea. He pointed to a spot along the cliff face.

"She was running along there, toward the main beach. The two men appeared behind her from around that rocky outcropping. The older of the two pulled a revolver and shot at the woman."

"Once?" I asked.

"No, there were two shots. I don't think the first one hit her. But on the second shot, the woman fell into the sand. The taller, younger seeming man, seemed very upset and ran to her. He carried her back in the direction they had come."

"Can you show us, as well as you remember, where the woman fell, Tony."

The boy nodded and led us to a sandy edge along the rocks.

"They shot from the water's edge over there," Tony said, pointing southeast. She fell here after the second shot."

Holmes walked over to the cliffside. His eyes scanned it for a time, then he pointed at a gouge in the stone. "The first bullet hit there, I'd say."

I nodded my agreement.

Holmes began a careful examination of the sand where Tony had indicated he saw the woman fall. It wasn't long before he cried, "Watson!"

I made my way over. Holmes held a clump of sand stuck together in a brownish lump.

"Blood," I said. "Dried blood." I broke the clump up with my fingertips. The blood was not completely dried in the center. I looked at Holmes, "I'd like to tell this Marlowe a thing or two."

"I think we should hold off on that Watson."

I looked at Holmes. There was a familiar gleam in his eye. He turned to young Tony.

"You say the men came from this direction?" he asked, pointing to the edge of rock."

Tony nodded.

We found what resembled a rough path heading around the edge of the jutting stone. Holmes bade Tony to remain behind, and the boy obeyed. We made our way around the corner and followed the path along the stone to the cliff wall. Beneath us, the sea crashed and sent up spray that slicked the rocks. The trail led to a section of cliff that resembled a natural doorway. Holmes spent some time examining the stone, his fingers carefully tracing tracks. Finally, he stood up.

"It's a doorway, Watson. To what, I don't know. But I can find no way to open this doorway from this side."

I lifted my eyes upward and followed the cliff. Over the top of the cliff, smoke drifted out as if from a chimney.

"I think we need to visit the owner of the house at the top of the cliff."

"Indeed, Watson. indeed!"

114

We dropped young Tony off with his parents, and Holmes promised to let him know what we discovered. The boy had, on our walk back, given as detailed as possible a description of both the two men and the woman they were pursuing. On the way back across the beach, Holmes, Tony, and I had gotten a good look at the mansion that stood at the top of the cliff above the secret doorway to the beach. It was a sprawling affair that once bespoke of wealth. But the state of disarray of the mansion, missing roof tiles, flaking paint, indicated that wealth may have existed in the past, and current times were not nearly as rosy.

"We must find out as much as we can about that mansion," Holmes observed.

Knowing Holmes's methods, I said, "I think we passed two pubs on the way in."

Holmes smiled, "Excellent thinking, Watson. Perhaps at one of the pubs, I can send a message to my brother Mycroft."

We made our way to the nearest pub, the Golden Boar. The proprietor was a red-headed Irishman named Finnegan who introduced himself to us and stared at us blankly with his mouth agape when we identified ourselves.

Finally, he leaned in toward us and whispered, "Are you here to investigate the goings-on at Colonel Mustard's?"

Holmes only nodded to the question, saying, "I have an urgent need to use your telephone."

After he had used the phone, he joined me at the bar. "Mycroft wasn't in, but I was able to leave a message," Holmes said to me. He turned to Finnegan. "If a call comes for me, will you make sure I get the message?"

"Anything for you, Mr. Holmes."

Finnegan told us everything we wanted to know about the mansion. It turned out that the man occupying it was a grandson of Lord Mustard. Mustard had become extremely wealthy in the slave trade at the turn of the last century and had built the mansion in 1836. The grandson, who demanded people call him Colonel, was not much liked in Blackpool. He did almost no business at all with the locals, and neither did his visitors. The goings-on that Finnegan described amounted to nothing more on the face of it other than odd visitors during the night. But according to Finnegan, the activities seemed suspiciously secretive.

"My own father knew Lord Mustard personally. He'd come to the pub and buy a round for the boys," Finnegan said. "But somehow there was a falling out in the family and the one that got the mansion here, the Colonel as he likes to be called, does have naught to do with his royal kin," Finnegan said, sarcastically. "If you wanted to question him, you are right out of luck. He took off this morning in his carriage. Only his manservant, Oliver, will be at the mansion. Nobody likes him either. I am pretty sure the man is a Kraut.

"Could Marlowe, the local policeman, be in on whatever Mustard is up to?" I asked.

Just then, an old man entered the tavern. "Be right with you," he called to the customer.

Finnegan gripped Holmes' arm, pulled him close and whispered. "They are as thick as thieves."

Outside the pub, we found Tony Pratt waiting for us. I thought Holmes would admonish the boy, but instead, he asked, "Were you wearing the same clothes when you saw the men chasing the woman?"

"No, Mr. Holmes. I was wearing a bathing outfit."

"Did they get a good look at you?"

"They were concentrating on the woman. I don't think they ever saw me."

"Good, then it will be safe for you to deliver a message for me."

Not long after, Holmes and I were hidden in the trees watching young Pratt walk toward the mansion.

"What did you write in your note?" I asked.

"Utter nonsense, precisely: Due to international conditions, delivery cannot be made until Thursday next. With scribbling as the signature."

"To what purpose?" I asked.

"I want a look at this Oliver before we approach the mansion itself.

Pratt was almost to the door, and Holmes produced his opera glasses. "Now, we'll see just what this English servant looks like."

We watched Tony sound the doorbell. Some minutes later, the door was opened by a tall man with dark hair. The man took the note from the boy and read it quickly. From his expression, the letter made no sense. As instructed, Tony held out his hand for a tip. The man reached into his pocket and gave what he retrieved to Tony.

Out of sight of the mansion, he approached Holmes and I.

"Was that one of the men you saw at the beach?" Holmes asked.

"Yes, sir. He was the one who ran to help the woman after she was shot."

"You are a brave boy, Mr. Pratt. I envision great things for you. But for now, I want you to go back to

your family and stay with them, and do not come anywhere near this mansion again."

"Yes, sir. But you will let me know the result of your
inquiry?"

"That we will do," Holmes said.

"What will we do now?" I asked Holmes after young
Pratt had left us.

"I think the first stop is a haberdashery," Holmes
said.

An hour later, Holmes was a changed man. Dressed in
black, with a pince-nez, he looked more like a servant
of the Kaiser than the Queen. Since I did not have my
medical bag, he had purchased a similar bag that
would serve.

We drove to the mansion in an expensive-looking au-
tomobile Holmes had somehow procured. I stood next
to him as he sounded the bell at the door of Colonel
Mustard's mansion. It was not long before the tall and
intimidating form of Oliver, Mustard's manservant,
stood before us.

"Yes," he asked suspiciously as he took the two of us
in.

"Von Bork," Holmes said, sternly, with a pronounced
German accent. "Don't just stand there; let us inside
before someone sees."

Dumbfounded, the giant moved aside, and we
rushed in.

"Shut the door," Holmes instructed even as the man
was doing so.

"Headquarters is concerned the female captive may not live until the U-boat can retrieve her. Thus I have brought this doctor."

The big man turned to me. His expression took me by surprise, for it seemed one of pure joy at my being there.

"This way," he said without hesitation. He led us to the library, where he tipped a book out on a large bookcase against the wall and stepped back. There was a mechanical sound, and the bookcase swung outward. He reached inside and took an electric lantern off the wall and turned it on.

"This leads to the stairway to the cavern," the big man said. Then rushed ahead to lead the way. We had to ascend a very steep staircase that wound its way through stone until we reached a level floor far below the mansion.

"This way," the big man said. He led us to a stone room where chains had been set in the wall. The woman lying on the floor was not chained. She had been laid out on a blanket with a jacket folded under her head. Sweat beaded on her pale skin.

"Monique," the big man said, tenderly, "I have brought help."

"Out of my way," I said, and he made way willingly. The woman's forehead was on fire. "How long has she been this way?"

"Two days now," the man said with feeling. "She was shot."

"Mustard shot her?" Holmes cried in his German accent. "The fool! What was he thinking?" He turned to the big man and asked. "When is the submarine due?"

"Tomorrow night," the man said.

My focus was on the woman. She had been shot in the upper thigh. The bullet had not pieced an artery or

119

a vein, but the wound had puffed up, inflamed. The gauze I removed was soaked in puss.

"But she will not be getting on the submarine," the man said.

I looked up to see him now holding a gun on Holmes. As I looked at him, he waved the pistol at me.

"You," he said, indicating me, will help her. It is worth your life."

I had every intention of saving the woman's life if I could. Still, my regret now was the empty bag we had purchased to mimic a medical bag, and sorely wished I had my real one.

Then the man turned to Holmes. "You, I have no further use for. "

"Oh, but I think you do, Oliver," Holmes said, now speaking with his normal voice. "You deliberately let the woman escape the other day. It was unfortunate that the man you work for discovered her missing and began the chase before she could get away."

The man just stared at Holmes.

"Besides, your origins are Dutch, not German. So I imagine you were somehow recruited when you were younger.

"I am Sherlock Holmes," Holmes said. "This is my friend and chronicler, Dr. John Watson. Perhaps you have heard of us."

The man nodded, indicating he had heard of my colleague. "But how are you here?"

"I just captured Von Bork. We were taking a holiday when a boy who witnessed the shooting of the woman told me the story. I assume the local constable is controlled by the man calling himself Colonel Mustard?"

"He is a German agent. He waylaid the real constable as the man was traveling here to begin the job. That was some years ago." The big man looked at both of us. I was sent here years ago to work with Colonel Mustard. But I have no real tie to Germany. As a young man, I loved a woman who lived in Berlin. She died tragically, and in my despair, I joined the German army. I worked under the officer who recruited Colonel Mustard, who sent me here to spy on him as well as aid him. But I have grown to love this country. I have been thinking of defecting for some time." He lowered his pistol. "I wish to surrender to Mr. Sherlock Holmes and Dr. Watson. But, please, Dr. Watson. Do what you can to save this woman. I have grown very fond of her."

With the local constable, a German agent, our choices were limited. After a phone call to Sherlock's brother, Mycroft: we let Hanz Widmark, which was Oliver's real name, take Monique to the hospital. We learned later that he did turn himself in to British agents at the hospital and was of much help later in supplying information about German spies in the country.

But first, we had to deal with Colonel Mustard. Hanz told us that Mustard would be arriving back that evening. It was his usual procedure to check on the prisoner as soon as he arrived.

Holmes and I were seated in the library, in the dark, with a good view of the only door. About 9 o'clock that evening, we heard the door of the mansion open.

"Oliver?" a gruff voice cried. When there was no response, he called out again, louder this time, "Oliver?"

Footsteps came rapidly toward the library after that. Before leaving, Hanz had shown us the mansion's armory. I was armed with a pistol. It was in the pocket of my coat. It pointed in the direction of the doorway when the tall, grey-haired figure of Colonel Mustard, turned on the electric lights and stormed into the library shouting, "Oliver!"

"I am afraid Hanz is not here," Holmes said. "Nor is your guest."

In a duet of movement, both men moved with lightning speed. So swiftly, I barely saw his hand move Mustard suddenly had a revolver pointed at Holmes. Holmes, moving so rapidly as to be a blur, picked up a candlestick on the table next to him and threw it like a war club. Almost at the same time, there was a gunshot. Thinking that Mustard had shot Holmes, I fired my own pistol. But it took only a second to see, as the sound of my gunshot faded that Mustard had already been falling. Holmes' candlestick had struck first. Holmes jumped up and kicked the gun away. I went to the fallen spy. But there was nothing to do for him. The right side of his skull was caved in. My bullet had pierced his black heart.

"He was as dangerous as I suspected, Watson," Holmes said moments later. "I was lucky."

We had to extend our stay to make it seem life was going on at the mansion as usual. Mycroft's men could not risk the arrest of Officer Marlowe until the next evening.

It was immediately after a German U-boat was destroyed by British Torpedoes just a mile off the beach that Marlowe was arrested and charged with treason.

We met Tony Pratt for the last time the next day. The family was heading home. Exploding U-boats in the night did not make for a peaceful holiday. We did, as promised, bring Tony Pratt up to date on the adventure.

"So it was Mustard, in the library with the candlestick," I remembered Tony saying before we made our goodbyes. For some reason, those words stuck with me.

—The End—

www.ingramcontent.com/pod-product-compliance
Lightning Source LLC
Chambersburg PA
CBHW030545130626
46552CB00006B/2436